Dear Venny, De

Gary Crew is a lecturer in Creative Writing and is Chair of The Queensland Writer's Centre. He has won various literary prizes including the Children's Book Council of Australia, Book of the Year for Older Readers, and the American Children's Book of Distinction.

Libby Hathorn is the author of many outstanding novels for children and young adults. Her multitude of awards include the Society of School Librarian's International Honour Book, and the American Library Association Best Book for Young Adults. Her titles frequently appear in American and Australian children's Best Book and Honour Book listings.

Gary Crew & Libby Hathorn

Dear Venny, Dear Saffron

Flyways

First published in 1999 by Thomas C. Lothian Pty Ltd,
Port Melbourne, Australia.
First British edition published in 2000 by Flyways,
an imprint of Floris Books

British Library CIP Data available

ISBN 0–86315–331–3

Printed in Great Britain
by Creative Print & Design, Harmondsworth

*For all those who love the
adventure of writing*

LH & GC

Letter 1

12 Acacia Drive
Springvale Qld 4035
Australia

5 March

Dear Miss Saffron Duval

I am writing this letter to you because my english teacher Mr Duncan says everyone in our class has to have a pen friend as part of our english course this year.

Mr Duncan says that he met your english teacher at a conference in New York last year and they set up this idea. I think it is dum idea because I don't like writing but I have to do it or else I will fale english and my parents would crack up and I would be grounded.

Mr Duncan says that I have to introduce myself and tell you about myself and where I live and my friends and my hobbys. He says that this letter should make me sound interesting so that you would want to write back to me.

I have to write 500 words or else Mr Duncan will make me do it all over again. He says we can write anything we like as long as it makes sensce.

But you don't have to write back to me if you don't want to then I can tell Mr Duncan that my pen friend did not want to be in the deal and coped out. OK?

Anyway, since I have to do this, the first thing is that my name is Venny Merlo and I am 16 years old. I don't want to tell you my middle name because it really sux. I am in Year 10 at Springvale State High School.

I am not a good student but I do what I have to do so my parents wont crack up. The subjects that I do at school are: english (yuk) maths (yuk yuk) science (OK sometimes) geography (OK because you get to go outside and look at clouds sometimes) manual arts (OK) art (I can't draw anything but I like mixing up paint and slapping it on and I like mucky clay) and drama. I have to take drama because the only other choice was to take home economics (H.E. is cooking and sewing). Girls do h.e. but there is one boy called Dwayne who takes it because he wants to be a chef. No boys talk to Dwayne. I would because I like food and I think that he is a brave dood to do it but I don't think that Dwayne wants to talk to me anyway.

I don't have any hobbys but I have a lot of friends and we skateboard in the carpark behind the 24 hour convenience store at the Springvale Shopping Centre.

Well, boys in this country don't really have friends. They have what we call mates. My best mates name is Joel. He's a cool dood. He lives down the road in Banksia Drive.

I live with my dad who is a panel beater and spray painter in a car body shop and my mum who works in a cold room packing meat. My sisters name is Teresa. Joels got a sister called Marcia like in the Brady Bunch on TV. Both our sisters are ten years old. Everyday they do there hair a different way but it always looks dum.

And even uglier if that's possible. They also do the hair on there *My Little Ponies* tales.

My house is made of wood and has got brick foundations and 3 bedrooms and a patio. I've got my own bedroom. I like Kurt Cobain. He is (was) a dood but since he is dead now I have stuck his poster on the wall in my bedroom.

Mr Duncan says that we should ask you questions about yourself. Here is my first question.

1. What do you look like?
2. Another question is have you got a skateboard?

If you write back to me I might tell you what I look like, but you don't have to write back like I said.

I have written more than 500 words already so I will sign off now.

Yours in my doodness

Venny Merlo (Dood)

Letter 2

The Penthouse
511 Park Ave
New York NY 10017

April 12

Dear Venny

An unusual name, but so is Saffron, I guess. I'm sorry I've taken a few weeks to answer. I know my tutor and your teacher set up this pen pal idea, but he (my tutor) also got me to place an ad. for a pen pal in an international kids' magazine.

I had five replies and of course your letter. I must admit, I answered Marvin's first. What a mistake! Marvin E.J. Barker — this jerk of a guy — turns up at our apartment and asks me for a date. Turns out he lives on the east side and he's not interested in being a pen pal at all, but likes the sound of a Park Avenue address! Never mind, my aunt and I will be going travelling in about a month, so I won't be seeing that Snake-eyes in a long time (which is a relief — talk about an ego!).

So, coming back to the other four writers — I worked out Park Avenue probably won't mean a thing to someone in Springvale (sounds lovely — like deep in the woods or something), Australia, and that's just great by me, and by Aunt Beatrice I guess.

Beatrice, as in Great Aunt, was furious when

Captain Marvel (as I called Marvin E.J.) turned up in a spotted yellow tie and grotty old jogging shoes (he had other clothes on of course). She was furious that I hadn't listed our post-office-box address, which I'll give you (that is if you haven't already had 100 offers of pen pals by now yourself).

I chose you, Venny, from the other four (OK second choice is not the best, but it's better than fifth) because I liked some of the things you said. They sounded a bit nerdy — don't get offended — about having to write the letter like a punishment, but then doing it! And I like it that you admire that chef boy at school (I like cooking too) and best of all that you don't like school. I can see you don't like spelling. Want a tip? Look, I'm not the best speller in the world but your computer has a thing called "Spellcheck." Sometimes it can give funny substitutions for words — like "Beatrice" becomes "Boatrace," (and " dum" in your letter on my spellcheck suggests "doom"). But often it's useful in just giving you the right spelling — e.g. "dum" should be "dumb!" Don't worry too much — it's kind of cute you spell like that. And I feel I can tell you things like that because you are a year younger than I am — another reason for my choice. (You won't be as likely to try to crack on to me or anything — well, you won't be like Marvin.)

As I said, I liked it that you didn't like school! I hated school so much I was once going to run away from home. (Got as far as the Village, outside my favourite foodstore on Broadway. That's Dean and Deluccas, where Aunt Beatrice always shops.) Anyhow, Beatrice's limo pulls up and her driver motions me to the kerb. He'd been trailing me for the whole 40 blocks I'd skateboarded. He said I'd probably had enough exercise and it was getting dark. He had a point — I didn't have a clear plan and I was getting kinda hungry, so I got back in the car, went home to Park Avenue and had a deep-and-meaningful with Beatrice. The first of many. Things got better after that, but I still had to go to school!

I guess I'd better explain who Beatrice is. She's my great aunt (on my father's side) and my only living rel. She was once the toast of New York, Paris and Rome, according to her antique girlfriend, Françoise Proust, who hangs out here with us a lot. Beatrice was married to a banker who died way back, leaving her lots of dough. When my Mom was killed three years ago, well, there was no one else in the world for me.

Beatrice didn't want me and I didn't want Beatrice, but she felt duty-bound and said we could have a three-month trial period where I stayed in her apartment. (Otherwise she'd have put me in a posh boarding school.) It's now three years on and, yes, we have an understanding. Don't get me wrong — I like her lots, but she can be a dog! She's the strongest, most resolute person I've ever known, eighty-something or not.

Talking of dogs, she was merciless about my dog Spaghetti. I had this mutt — a shaggy little number with the cutest way of putting his head on one side when you talked to him. Beatrice wouldn't allow Spaghetti to come and live in her apartment, even though lots of old dears in this block have their "toy" dogs. It was our first fight, and she won! Saying good-

14

bye to Spaghetti was just the worst — I still haven't got over it and I probably never will.

Back to my unsuccessful school days. Most of the kids at my school are painful in the extreme. They know I'm an orphan and some of them have made me pay for that. Or they know Beatrice is ultra-loaded and they kind of suck up to me. The counsellor thinks I'm inclined to be paranoid, but you try to put up with New Yorker girls at a posh school for longer than the duration of a movie and it just plain sucks.

So, I was relieved when Beatrice hired a tutor for me. Notice I said was relieved. He has turned out to be the king of nerds. Maybe he and Mr Duncan are a good pair. Kevin (Kevin, imagine!) Millass. I've named him Kevin Bypass or just plain Ass (with "hole" added under my breath).

Hey, I didn't mean to go on like this at all! I'm already telling you personal things and I don't even know you!

Are you interested in getting a kind of travelogue of letters from me? Beatrice, who is always mysterious (launches off into French with the ancient Françoise when she wants to say private things in front of yours truly), made an announcement a month ago.

Aunt Beatrice and I are going to leave this very pleasant pad of hers, she tells Françoise and me, and go on a jaunt that might take up to a year!

"We'll be visiting some strange, even weird places, I have to warn you, Saffron," she said, with a certain look in her eye that I like. She added that she was hiring a tutor for me, who was to be with us most of the time. And she said I'd have to be prepared for a lot of change.

I jumped at the idea. Who wouldn't? I asked her fifty-four questions, none of which she answered satisfactorily. Basic ones like, "Where exactly are we going?" that got infuriating answers like, "You'll see," "And why are we going?" "Several reasons."

So I decided the whole thing would be a kind of quest for me. Talk about a journey of discovery! If I come back knowing why an old lady, who is kicking back very comfortably, thanks, in her New York apartment, would undertake a year-long journey to some weird and uncomfortable places — if I come back knowing why, then I've succeeded in understanding something about Beatrice Duval I didn't know before. I have to ask and ask to dig info. out of her.

Thank God for Françoise, who's a mine of information if I can get her alone. She's already hinted that she knows that our first stop is not even off this continent, but it's an exciting one — LA! Maybe I'll get to see Warner Brothers or Fox Studios or Dreamworld, never mind Kevin the tutor! Françoise, by the way, is minding the apartment while we're gone.

So, if you want to come with me, Venny (are you sure you spelt it right and it's not Veni?) then this is an invitation. (Veni, vidi, vici = I came, I saw, I conquered. Yes, I have studied two dead languages — Ancient Greek and equally ancient Latin. Of any interest? Hmm, I guess not!)

Let me know pretty quickly if you want to be my pen pal or I'll have to go to No. 3, a Fenella Jane Collingsworth, who sounds a bit of a pain.

Yes, I have a skateboard, as I said already, and you'll

just have to imagine what I look like for the moment.
(I'm not a film star or anything, but I'll send a photo
later, maybe.) Can you send me a photo of you (and
Teresa)?

Best wishes to you Down Under

Saffron

Plee-ee-ease forget the Miss bit! It makes me feel so
old.

Letter 3

19 May

Dear Ms Saffron Duval

You sure do write weird letters. I mean, I reckon what you said about me learning to use the spell check on the computer was bad. I wrote that letter to you in class time and the period ended before I had a chance to use it. OK? Course I can use a spell check.

Yeah, OK, so we have both got dumb names but I don't reckon there nearly as dumb as that guy Marvin's name. Reminds me of the name of that singer Marvin Gaye. He must have been one brave dood. You know?

No, Springvale isn't lovely like you think and there sure aren't any woods nearby. There's just a bit of straggly bush next to the rubbish tip. In fact, Springvale sux. It's a suburb where people who don't have much money can afford a cheap house of their own. But my mum and dad reckon that living here and paying off there own house is better than living in an apartment (like you call them) in some glitzy suburb and paying rent. That's chuckin' good money away, my dad says. He reckons he's not gonna keep some chardonnay-sippin' landlord fat.

You said that you tried to run away from home one time. Well, even though our place isn't so great and I don't like school much, I don't reckon that I would ever shoot through because my mum and dad are great, even though my sister is a pain in the you know where.

I reckon from reading your letter that my life is probably a fair bit different from yours. You said that you lived with your old aunty because your mum got killed but you didn't say how she got killed and you didn't say anything about your father, but you did say your an orphan so he probably is dead. Is he dead or was he a moron who shot thru on you and your mum? Is it alright if you tell me how your mum got killed or is it asking a bit much? You don't have to tell me if you don't want to. OK?

You're lucky to have a tutor even if he is a jerk. I wouldn't like to have a name like his either. When you called him Millass you reminded me that we got this new art teacher, a man called Willis. We started to call him Willass. Funny that, hey? A coincidence. But anyway when he turned out to be OK we stopped. Now we just call him Sir. He is different from other art teachers. He told us that he can't draw either and we do photography and what he calls "built structures." Photography is OK but theres not much equipment so you have to share and that sux like you can't work by yourself and do your own thing. You can't be independent.

But built structures is good. You have to scrounge around at home or in the tip (which is right near our house) and find old bits of steel and broken things like old vacuum cleaners and parts of old stereos and motor mowers and stuff like valves out of old radios. Then you bring them to school and Sir helps you arrange them into fantastic kinds of shapes that look cool.

Then you use glue to make them stay in that shape or structure. Sometimes we get the portable welder from the Manual Arts Workshop and weld parts together. I really like that.

One thing I made Sir has taken away to get chromed. It's kind of like a jaguar or a puma about to spring. In fact I even used some old springs for its leg mussels, which are exposed like the animal has no skin and you can see all its sinews and leg mussels. I made its ribs out of a pair of stainless steel blades from a food slicer. They look like silver combs and their teeth are really thin and even. I pressed the combs to make them curved like the two sides of a rib cage. The jaguar is about 30 cm long and 15 high. Sir said it is amazing. It will look a lot better still when it's chromed all over. Too cool.

You say that you are going travelling with your old Aunty. I don't think that I would like to travel much. We go to the coast for our holidays and I surf a bit. There's good surf in a lot of Australia but I'm not a real good surfer. I reckon that could be because my hair is dead black — the wrong colour, you know.

The best thing of all would be if I had my own wheels (car) and was able to drive up and down the coast whenever I wanted and not have to wait for a ride with dad or mum or one of my mates when he goes. If you have to go with someone you don't have any independence. I mightn't like to travel too much but I sure like my independence, hey.

My mum really worries about me having an accident in my mates' car. That's also why she's not keen on me getting my driver's licence either. She reckons that she had a premonition (used the spell check on that one) that something would happen to me going to the coast one day. I said, "Yeah, mum. I might pick up Elle McPherson hitch-hiking." My dad says, "You wish."

Anyway, that sounds OK like when you say would I like to come with you on your travels. That would be OK because then I could travel without leaving home. Sure. You can write about that, but don't go on and on about it will you, because it's sure to get dead boring if you're just describing old towns and gardens and stuff. You know?

Yeah, sure you can send me a photo of you but I'm not sending you one of me until I see yours first. That's what we call "you show me yours and I'll show you mine" over here in Oz (which is what some people call Australia. Pretty funny, eh?).

Anyway writing to you this time was alright so you can write to me again when you send me the photo. Alright?

From

King Venny of Oz Land

(Too cool. Yeah!)

Letter 4

Château Marmont
Sunset Boulevard
Hollywood, Los Angeles
90069 CA
USA

August 22

Dear King Venny
    Forget the "Ms" too!
    To tell you the truth I was very glad to receive your letter. Françoise is forwarding the mail and I couldn't believe there was a letter waiting for me when we got to LA. I'm doubly pleased because Aunt Beatrice is acting strange. (More than usually strange, I mean.) And already I'm feeling a bit lonely. (Bypass isn't joining us until France.) No more early morning walks in Central Park checking out the dogs there (looking for Spaghetti, of course). I've made friends with a Dalmatian and a German Shepherd and a Rottweiler, among the other canines who come by at different times — and yes, their owners as well! We talk dog talk mainly, and I miss all that.
    Look, I'm sorry about all the Spellcheck stuff. It

makes me sound like a pain, which I'm not! (depending on who you ask). I'm not even weird, even if you say I write weird letters! But I take this maddening interest in words — it drives me crazy sometimes. When I was little I spent a lot of time alone, and I read heaps and heaps of books from the library near us and it meant I got kind of hooked on words at an early age. So I can't help it, it's kind of a hobby ...

Your jaguar sounds just great — you could send a picture of that if you wanted. And your life — going on holidays with family and the way you like being with your Mom and Dad — that sounds great to me, even if Springvale isn't too lovely when you're at home. (I agree with your Dad about rent, my Mom would have said the same thing. But I think your Dad would probably like Beatrice's apartment.)

It made me feel a bit funny to hear you say all that about your folks (even your sister). But I'm glad you're writing to me again and it's not goddamn Fenella Jane.

My Dad took off before I was born, even though he came back a few times to haunt Mom. Then he got himself killed, when I was about five. A car crash on a snowy road, Mom said. He froze to death and I don't really care one bit, because I don't think he gave a rat's arse about Mom or me.

About my Mom — I might tell you stuff, but not just now. To tell you the truth, Venny, I'm trying not to think about her and about my life back there with her. (That was in a trailer park, more or less in the desert, so you can see it was very different from now.) It's a bit like

23

ground glass, the feeling back there, so I just close the book, if you know what I mean.

I'm not going to give you a travelogue or anything like it, so don't worry about that. But yesterday was cool. We went shopping down Rodeo Drive, and shopping with Aunt Beatrice when she's in the mood has to be the most amazing experience there is. She wanted a briefcase, so of course you start by looking in the most expensive street in the USA! She had a bee in her bonnet and we went in and out of so many shops. The briefcase had to have a security lock, blah, blah, blah.

Anyway, she found this pigskin case, very elegant with Fort Knox locks, and then on impulse she bought this cool bag I'd been admiring while she did the deal with the shop assistants. She's the label queen, so it had to be Prada or Versace or Chanel or whatever — and who am I to complain? I've got to admit my present is the coolest little backpack you ever saw — not showy one bit. It came complete with a mobile phone, only I've got no one much to call. Françoise, or maybe Lisette — she's kind of my friend from school.

Then we go and have coffee on Sunset Strip and I star-spot and I swear that I see Nicole Kidman, but Aunt Bea isn't so sure. Some ritzy-looking people go by and Aunt says most of them are would-be's-if-they-could-be's in the movie world. Maybe this sounds a bit pretentious to you, but life with Aunt Bea is! Only it's real.

Anyway, then Bea goes into a mood. Back to the

hotel. We're staying in a château (as one does). Well it's a Hollywood-version, fake château — a place where stars stayed in the 30s — nearly every star you've ever heard of from the Golden Years, and it's the "in" place again or my great aunt would not be here. The lawyers from the O.J. Simpson case holed up here during the trial and somebody from the rock era (can't remember his name) killed himself here too!

We have a suite on the top floor and it was once inhabited by Howard Hughes, the millionaire. Instead of being happy here, with a view to the hills and the swimming pool downstairs — Bea gets grumpy and preoccupied and she stays on the phone for hours and tells me I can't go out because we're probably going to a meeting any minute.

I get down to the pool eventually anyway, and meet this great guy, John, and guess where he's from? Australia! He's not young or anything, and his wife is around somewhere, but he's friendly and easy to talk to and jokes around a lot. And he was a surf lifesaver! Anyway, I like him and wish Aunt Beatrice was going to a meeting with him. Is everybody that laid back down there?

One meeting? Next day we do Ventura Boulevard, Studio City — meeting after meeting, and I don't think it's exciting at all. A lot of old guys in suits who smile at me and then disappear with her and I begin to think maybe she's going to make a movie and she's fixing it so I get a bit part. I'm left reading the latest Hollywood Today mag. But she comes out of every meeting so glum it can't be she's doing anything fun.

And it's maddening that she won't tell me what's going on. Well, she does, but only in dribs and drabs.

'I'm looking for an old friend," she finally said in the afternoon, after I'd asked twice, "and I hope you like jazz, Saffron."

"Why?" I ask.

'We're going to House of Blues tonight. That's after dinner.'

'Is he playing there?'

That's it. She doesn't answer. Just rearranges papers she's collected from the movie dudes and puts them into the pigskin briefcase. Then says tartly to me, "What makes you think it's a he? It's a family friend, and that's all I want to say."

This gives me a bit of a jolt — I mean I like jazz, but I couldn't say I love it.

House of Blues is on the next corner and it's this corrugated iron shack like in the deep south — a very happening place to go (so who am I to complain?). But she only ever mentions family on bad days and it makes me think of my Mom, and even my Dad. And that glassy feeling creeps up on me again. So I go into my room, where they leave a movie script by every bed. Honest! They do! And I throw myself on the bed and read the script of "Casablanca" from cover to cover. Pretty mushy, but not bad reading.

It's not really true that I don't care about my Dad. I keep this old photograph in my wallet of him and Mom at a dance. My Mom looks beautiful in a swirly dress. She was beautiful then, which, sad to say, is not the way I remember her. I always think fate is cruel because I don't look like her when she was young, not one little bit. And my Dad looks interesting. Not specially handsome, but his eyes — he has doe eyes, they look so deep. Despite everything Mom's told me about him (none of it real good), I wish I'd had the chance to know him. Even just to see him, now I'm grown up. (Well, almost.)

Hey, what is this, Venny? You've done it again! Making me tell you things I don't really set out to tell you — or anyone.

You would love this place for the limos — and yes, Aunt Beatrice is going to hire one, with a driver, because tomorrow we're going to the hills. It's the house of a friend, next door to Madonna's, she says, and we're visiting! She says we can go to the Santa Monica beach, too, if it's warm. Maybe I'll get to surf.

With Aunt Beatrice, a bad mood is inevitably followed by a good one.

I forgot to tell you that she hired Kev the tutor because, among other things, he was once a specialist art teacher. She figures I have "talent with a paintbrush." When I was acting nerdy a while back, this analyst that Beatrice had me see said that maybe I should try to express my feelings in some other way than words, and why not try painting? I did and I liked it a lot. Françoise then pronounced that I had "raw talent" and Beatrice decided I should get training. She does like everything to be in jars you can put a lid on, but she means well, I s'pose. See, I like the idea of your "built structure," which sounds like a happening *piece, much freer and more of an experiment than painting on a small canvas. I want to work on really large canvasses one day. That's freedom to me. Anyway, when we get to France (which is our next stop, apparently — we're going to stay a while in Normandy), I'm looking forward to painting (as well as Maths lessons from the tutor). There's just so much shopping you can do — joke!*

I feel your Mom shouldn't say things like that premonition about your driving and going to the coast. I mean, doesn't it kind of set you up? See, I don't thin k we can control much of what happens to us — just make these feeble attempts. Like Beatrice is making now. Mind you she can change countries at will, so I guess that is some control. But not really. Not in the Big Way, or else she'd never be sad the way she can be, despite all her money!

Well, I'm not sad tonight. I'm out on the balcony finishing this before we go out to our jazz club. (Isn't it funny — Beatrice reminded me just then that I'm s'-posed to be writing to my pen pal, as if it's a kind of duty.) I just smiled and nodded and looked mysterious. (Well, I tried to.)

I have a mutt with me. The head waiter from the groovy club next door where we had dinner has given me his collie dog on loan for an hour. He's at my feet right now (the dog, not the waiter).

It's warm and even way up here I can smell the flowers from down round the pool, I swear it. And collie dog! And, let's face it, exhaust fumes.

Mmmm. Lots and lots of traffic swishing by — a million tail lights up ahead — and all the glitzy neon of

LA is kind of shining round me. Without being too travelogue, it's kind of neat up here!

I'm enclosing my photo, which Françoise took for me. Guess who she caught me writing to??

With fond regards to a mate. (John told me they say mate in Oz Land. Is it too soon to call you that? Please tell me.)

Saffron

Letter 5

28 October

Dear Saffron

It was good to get your letter even though I didn't know half of what you were talking about. I had to go to the school library and look up where LA is in the atlas. At our school it's not cool for boys to go to the library, especially in their own free time, and if my mates found out I went there they would think that I was weird like that Dwayne who does Home Economics I told you about. Anyway, the sculpture of the jaguar I made in art is on show there so I said I was going to see that. It's hard to get away from my mates. We always stick together. In the end I went with my best mate Joel but he still thought I was weird when I looked up the atlas so I had to tell him about you. He is into baseball so it was OK to look up places in America, but he's very suss about me writing to a girl. But I am anyway.

No, girls can't be your mates, so don't say that.

That photo you sent me was pretty nice. You don't look like the girls at my school. Everyone over here has to wear a uniform to school and the girls have to wear straw hats. The teachers reckon that we will get skin cancer because of the bright sun. But the teachers don't wear hats. Funny that. I reckon the real reason for wearing a uniform is that the teachers think we are easier to control if we all look the same. Anyway, you look pretty good. You look like your own person. Like an individual. But sometimes it's hard to be an individual when you're with all your mates, you know?

I didn't really have to write back to you because that English teacher we had, Mr Duncan, the one who made us write the pen friend letters, he got the sack. Turns out that he had a girlfriend in Year 12. I didn't know her because she was a stuck-up perfect prefect, but Mr Duncan was also a Speech and Drama teacher and he used to throw parties for kids in Year 12 at his flat. Turns out that she used to stay the night and someone dobbed on them. That's the way it goes at school. You are really lucky you don't have to go. I can hardly wait to get out. I would like to be a panel beater and spray painter like my dad. There's always plenty of work and you're always moving around. I would hate to be stuck in an office sitting on my bum all day.

My mum says that's the way I will end up if I drive around with my mates. She says, "Take care in cars or else you'll end up in hospital." My mum can be seriously spooky. She can ruin a good weekend up the coast.

Anyway, now we've got this new English teacher called Miss Symes. She's alright but she's changed everything Mr Duncan was doing in English, most likely out of spite. Everyone reckons that she was jealous of his perfect girlfriend. She said we didn't have to write our pen friend letters any more. But I'm going to because I have this fill-in (pretend veggie) subject called

Computer Awareness. We only have to do it one period a week so it's a bit like Religious Education. You have to do it even if you don't want to but it's dumb. I was always in trouble because I didn't bring anything to do like an assignment to print out or something, so I am going to keep on writing to you to give me something to do. (I guess I could email you, only this school is too lousy to let us go on-line.) Anyway, I think writing to you is ok but I'm not telling my mates (except Joel of course) because if they knew they would bag me.

It was sad what you wrote about your family, especially your dad and mum. I guess I'm lucky. My mum and dad get on OK and don't have many fights. But they argue sometimes, especially when it's dad's fishing weekend with his mates. Mum reckons all they do is drink beer and get drunk. He never brings any fish home. Even I know that.

Your Aunty Beetroot or whatever her name is (I left your letter at home) sounds really weird. All my rellies live in Sydney and some are still in Italy so I don't see them much, but my dad's father is still alive. Grandpa is in Eventide — an old peoples home. We go to see him some Sundays. He's OK but I don't think he knows who I am. He's got Alzheimer's disease. (I spellchecked that one) like Bart Simpson's gramps on TV. Do you get to see the Simpsons over there? I watch some TV, especially the footy.

I don't read books like you do, only the ones like "To Kill a Mockingbird" that we have to read for school. It took me a whole semester to read but I did. It was OK. I liked the girl, Scout, because she was honest and smart. The theme of race prejudice came through very clear. That is a problem in Australia as well, especially fights between some property owners and the Aboriginies over land rights. Aboriginal people were living in this land before the whites came. I mean, my dad's dad only came over here from Sicily in the 1950s. I saw Mockingbird on video in my English class. It was in black and white but the whole class paid attention, which was weird.

We had to read "The Outsiders" as well but I thought that the character Ponyboy was really a girl like the author Susan Hinton so I gave it away, but I got it out and saw it on video which was better. Tom Cruise was really young then. Nicole Kidman is an Aussie. She's a babe but she looks a bit like she was a prefect, I reckon.

Did you really go to an analyst like a shrink on TV? Everyone on TV goes to a shrink. How come you needed to go? Were you shook up when your dad got killed? I know I would be. We can go to our school counsellor if we have a problem. I haven't been but my sister is a bed-wetter so she has had some help. We don't talk about her problem much at home but I know it goes on.

My mate Joel has had counselling from the school counsellor because he has ADD (not AIDS). ADD stands for Attention Deficit Disorder. He can't sit still and he's always fooling around in class. He's a great skateboarder but he is terrible in class. It's like he's got ants in his pants. He's on some sort of medication (tablets) and a special diet. No chocolate or slurpies. He doesn't stick to it all the time so he breaks out something crazy. But you should see him in Manual Arts. He's great at using tools and things.

Maybe I'm a bit like that, which is why I like art, especially making built structures like my jaguar where you bash stuff like metal bits and pieces. I like that. That's how come I want to be a panel beater too. Anyway I'm sorry you had to go to an analyst but if painting makes you feel better, that's good. If it helps you work out problems.

You're lucky that your aunty has got plenty of money. I don't really believe what people say about money not making you happy. It sure as hell helps, I reckon. There are millions of starving and homeless people in the world who would sure like to have a bit. Anyway, this period is over so I have to stop. Kids are staring at me because I've been head down bum up for 45 minutes. Oh well, there's a first time for everything.

Venny

PS. I forgot to say please don't call me King either. I shouldn't have written that. It was a dumb joke. My mum and dad say there was only one real King and that was Elvis. Maybe when you're watching all the film stars over there you might see him. Mum and dad reckon he's still alive. I don't really believe that but they are into the 50s and Country and Western Music. I don't believe that there should be kings and queens. I want Australia to be a republic. All those kings and queens are just worn-out old history. We should be positive and think of the future.

PPS. I will send you a photo of my jaguar that was in the school magazine. You will see me standing beside it. I have got a bit of bum fluff on my top lip. When dad saw the photo he bought me a razor so I had a shave. I look better now. I have to go because kids from the next class are coming into the room but I was wondering if you would send me a painting that you did. I want to know if they look psycho. I don't mean you look like that. (Sorry. But I was wondering.)

Letter 6

Ritz Carlton Hotel
Place de la Croisette
Cannes
France

March 7

Dear Venny

I'm sorry it's been so — hey, I said to myself I'd never begin a letter or a conversation with those words! So I'll begin again.

When we arrived at the airport here (in Cannes, France), an army band was playing in the terminal and I don't know why, but my aunt seemed very emotional.

"That damned music —," she said, "drums, bells and whistles," but I saw her eyes had a kind of veil.

"Makes me think of wartime," she said when she realized I knew she was upset.

"Mmm," was all I could say. I was irritated because they were playing American music and I could see it was an American band. We'd just arrived in France, for God's sake, and we're a long way from home! Besides which, I hate band music — too strident. I dislike airports too, I've decided, even the duty-free parts where Beatrice spends so much time.

What on earth can she have left to buy?

36

"Presents!" she announces when she sees that look on my face. She's always accusatory when I have the slightest look of disgruntlement (if there is such a word, which I'm sure there's not, but it fits my feelings perfectly).

We spent a whole month in Hollywood, which was fine for her and not that bad for me. I saw every movie in town and Kevin (tutor) did not join us. How lucky can you be?

I was so excited to be finally going abroad! Bea had said we were to stay in the French countryside, where we'd unfortunately be re-united with Bypass. But then, just before we boarded the plane, she said there'd been a change of plan and we'd be staying in Cannes a while. So I was a bit miffed, because I'd been imagining forests and farmhouses, châteaux, black-and-white cows in verdant meadows and lots of horse-riding opportunities.

In our taxi from the Cannes airport I was sure we'd head for the hillside of villas we passed — they looked so splendid in the afternoon sunlight. Beatrice never tells me where we are to stay exactly — likes the surprise of it for me, she says. But I feel it's a bit of a power trip on her part. (The thing is, she does have the power in our relationship — well, almost all of it.) But the cab swept right by and pulled up at the Ritz Carlton on Place de la Croisette — a gorgeously "ritzy" hotel right on the sweep of a beautiful bay looking out to sea.

"Unfortunately, Saffron, it's not time for the film festival yet, but you're a lucky girl. It starts in a few weeks and we'll be in the heart of it," Bea announced.

This kind of cheered me, though I would have preferred horse-riding if she'd asked me, which she hadn't.

For the hotel, read wedding cake — beautiful exterior and grand old upmarket foyer with Persian carpets, extra shiny brass everywhere and divinely uniformed bellhops. The feeling of a genuine interior (as opposed to the fake ones of so many hotels) makes it like a minor marble palace. This place is the reason I almost began my letter with an apology — it's why I haven't written you in so long.

I don't know why, Venny, I'm not sure at all, but tonight I wanted very much to tell you what's happening here. Not so much about my aunt, although that's the usual mystery. We're hanging about here because of the film festival — there's someone she's itching to see. Unfortunately it's not Leonardo di Caprio or Matt Damon — it's a movie director. I overheard one of her conversations, or the end of it, the other evening and she was arranging to meet this director guy. Apparently he'll be staying here too next week.

Anyway, I don't want to go on about that. I want to talk about something weird and wonderful, if not amazing. And it's the complex as opposed to simple fact that I believe I've fallen in love! For the first time, too. Don't laugh — please don't laugh, because it's serious, at least for me. His name is Carlo and he's Italian from just across the border. He's a bellhop here and he's just the most wonderful person. We met at breakfast downstairs, or at least our eyes met through the glass wall of the dining room. (We have a French breakfast and French conversation every morning — my aunt's idea of "educating" me painlessly in French conversation — her idea of painless!)

Well, Bea was chatting away and he was carrying a pile of luggage to the lift. He paused for just a moment and looked at me through the glass wall and it was like nothing I've ever felt before. I guess it was like what you see in the movies. I felt like the glass was about to shatter, with our looks burning through it. I truly did! I couldn't eat my toasted muesli or my favourite chocolate croissants. I could scarcely speak again, much to Bea's annoyance, because I was so busy watching out for the comings and goings of that gorgeous bellhop.

Later, in our corridor upstairs, we came face to face. He must have been watching and waiting for the chance. Anyway, I didn't know what to say and nor did he, but somehow we managed introductions (he speaks English) and we made some kind of ridiculous small talk. My knees went kind of weak because up close he is even more drop-dead gorgeous than I imagined. He was very nervous about being seen, but he asked for my room number.

I spent the whole morning dreaming up a way to get him to carry stuff up to my room. Then it came to me — I could go shopping with the shopping queen! She'd already informed me what shops lay directly behind the Carlton. Fred's, Armani, Versace, Prada, Gucci, Hermes, Tiffany's and Christian Dior — the usual. I figured I could make sure Beatrice bought bulky stuff.

It worked! That afternoon when Aunt Bea was still down at reception and he brought the parcels up to our room, he asked me out (in his very precise English overlaid with Italian and French)!

Cannes is a small place and everyone promenades in the evening. He took me to a dear little restaurant at the top of the hill down the other end of the bay. It was very crowded and I saw quite a few of the guests from our hotel. That made me quite nervous, because I'd told Beatrice I was seeing a movie with another guest, a girl from the US we'd met briefly that morning.

There's a ruined castle up on the hill as well — crumbling and quaint, of course — and we lingered there afterwards. I hope you don't mind my telling you all this, but it's new ground for me. This feeling that I don't know Carlo and yet I've known about him all my life! I don't want to tell anyone back home because even my friends (if you can call them that) are just as likely to tell their Moms, who may tell Beatrice. So you're it, Venny! And you're not like one of my girlfriends who'd get jealous.

To continue ...

We walked back to the hotel along the promenade, hand in hand. Carlo couldn't take me to the door, for obvious reasons, but we had a long farewell down on the beach. The beach here is lined with restaurants and it's hard to find a private place, but we managed. So I want to stay here as long as I can and I'm being very agreeable to my aunt, I can tell you!

What a place! What a hotel! I love every part of it. I even love the cluster of maids in the corridor — they must have some kind of meeting-place outside my room. Anyway, they twitter away every morning and there's giggling. Maybe they know about my secret meetings with Carlo, though I doubt he'd say a word to them. I've decided I like the French language so much! It's so pretty it's like a song, even when they anglicize it. Well, it sounds like a song in their mouths. Not so the concierge, who speaks with all the arrogance of the most powerful and wealthy guests here. Carlo is terrified of him and I'm not surprised.

God, how that concierge fussed over a woman with two despicably dressed lap-dogs yesterday! (Yes, they dress them in fancy coats and have diamond-studded leashes.) Anyway the concierge rushed to help this woman with the dogs. That kind of figures — they say the French love their dogs more than their children — and hey, I've just evidenced that in the hotel lounge.

There was a small child in a gorgeous little tailored coat and wearing a very French, navy beret. He was a bored little boy whose parents were taking afternoon tea. I spoke to him briefly in my appalling French. He was pressing his little hands to the glass and looking out to the grey sea and sky outside, and this waiter kind of swooped down on him with a reprimand about dirtying the glass! Yet when the two lap-dogs — also obviously there for afternoon tea — started barking, the same waiter laughed indulgently and actually patted one of the dogs.

Look, I love dogs — and I must admit to patting a lap-dog or two myself while we've been here. But I was so mad I got up immediately and patted the little boy! Then his parents made him sit up on the chair. Poor kid!

God, I'm not talking about Carlo, am I? He's on leave at the moment, so he won't be around for a few days, but I'm thinking of him every minute. Except for these minutes, I guess, when I'm thinking about this letter and you.

We went to the home of Matisse this afternoon, at a place called St Paul de Varennes, not far from our hotel (by cab). For some strange reason it made me think of you and your sculptures. Art on every wall and a serene feeling in the gallery. I guess that's why I came home and wrote you after all this time!

I reread your last letter first. You see, I carry them with me! (I love the Auntie Beetroot nickname, but she'd be furious!) You are really a cute-looking boy, Venny! and I mean that, despite the hairy upper lip. You might not like this, but from your photo (one cool dude leaning against the wall like that), I think you have a sensitive face, and that's borne out lots of times by what you say in your letters. I like the way you are so honest — American kids wouldn't say what you do. Or not the kids I know, at least.

I'm glad you liked "To Kill a Mockingbird," and you're so right about the racial prejudice bit — it's still bad here (I mean in the US, not Cannes). But I'm surprised to hear that there's any prejudice in Australia. To tell you the honest truth I was under the impression the Aborigines had sort of died out and there were only a few actors around like that Ernie Dingo I've seen in films — and a few people on television. So I thought it wasn't an issue for you. I've never heard about land rights. Maybe it's a bit like the Indian reserves.

I'm not sure I enjoy the videos or movies of books like "To Kill a Mockingbird" because I like the images you get in your head from words. Somehow they don't ever seem to match up to the movies (for me, that is). But I must admit to watching the movie of "Sense and

Sensibility" when we were studying it, instead of reading the book! I got an A+ for my essay too — I could say thanks to Emma Thompson! Have you ever seen a video of a very old movie called "The Tin Drum?" (I've never read the book but the movie is very very good.)

I'm glad my letter made you go to the library, and I think you should tell your mates to stick it if you have to think of an excuse to go there! Joel sounds a good kind of friend and maybe that Dwayne is too. I'm glad you liked my photo. You're right about being an individual. I'm glad I look that way to you. Being with my Mom back in my trailer home days, when she was really bad (drinking and stuff) it was all I had to hang on to — the thought that I was me, not her and not my Dad, and I'd get through somehow. I was more determined the worse it got. That doesn't mean, by the way, that I didn't love my mother a lot. I did and I do. Her photograph is in my wallet and I look at her every morning of my life. I admit it, I talk to her sometimes, too. I've told her about Carlo as well.

Please don't think I don't want your letters just because I'm all caught up with being in love at the moment. I really need you to write me just like you have been. And tell me, have you ever felt you were in love? I'd like to know how guys feel about it. Even one who lives so far away! Am I getting closer?

With affection (may I say that?)
One starry-eyed

Saffron

PS. I'll send you one of my pictures when next I get to do some painting. Once we go to the countryside as promised. (And they are NOT "psycho!" Neither am I!)

PPS. My Mom loved Elvis too — and the Beatles and Dylan and Jimmy Morrison.

Letter 7

Dear Saffron

I was really surprised to hear from you. After my last letter I thought that maybe you would never write back. I thought maybe I asked you too many personal questions about your shrink and your dad who got killed. But when your letter came it was really good. I went red when I read the part where you said that I looked cool. I'm really not cool but people say I'm photo-genetic (in the right light).

I was glad to hear that you got in love but if this guy is a waiter, mightn't he be a bit of a dill? I mean does he wear tight black pants with a cumblebum around his waste? Yuk.

I haven't been in love but some of my mates have and they reckon you can get hurt, so watch out.

I had to go to the library with Joel again to look up where Cannes is in the atlas. It's in the south of France. Hey! Cool — not that I would want to go there. Anyway, what you said about my mate Joel is true. He's a good guy but it's getting so that I'm the only one who thinks so. I told you that he's got ADD and has all this counselling. Well, now he's got worse, especially since he stopped taking his pills. He reckons that pills are

45

only for mad people and he's not mad, like in asilum mad. I don't think he's mad either, just kind of crazy. He just gets off on acting the fool. It's school that gets to him. All the rules and having to sit still. He stirs up teachers on purpose and they bite every time. I reckon they should go to counselling, not because they have got ADD but to learn that it's best to ignore Joel when he gets high. He does stuff like making spit bombs out of paper that he chews up and spits at girls and that kid Dwayne who does Home Economics. Joel doesn't do anything behind people's backs, though. He doesn't try to hide anything. He misbehaves when the teacher is watching. Especially in Science.

We've got this cranky Science teacher called Mr Nudson but everyone calls him Nude Nut or just Nudo or even Mr Nudes because he is bald as an egg. I reckon that he is about 60 years old. Not that I'm against old people. I like old people, but not cranky old people.

Anyway Nudes has got this problem that my mum tells me is probably a genital hernia because there is this big lump down the leg of his trousers (if you know what I mean) and when he puts his leg up on a chair, like when he is standing beside your seat talking to you, then this great big lump is right in your face and it makes you feel sick because you can guess what it is but you can't stop looking! Anyway, Nudes is like Joel's pet hate and vicee-versee. Joel really stirs him. Last week in Science, Joel put these 2 boiled eggs on his desk and rolled them around and when Nudes told him to put them away Joel said, "Aw, sorry sir, I just keep them because they remind me of you." Nudes went ballistic (wow, I think I just cracked a pun!). I'm sure he must have known what Joel meant.

I would call Nudes asilum mad. I mean, any teacher who is that old and cranky (with his lumpy hernia things hanging down) who is still a teacher must be mad. He must have 1000s and 1000s of dollars in his teacher's retirement fund so I reckon he should retire to the beach, or something (but not wear bathers, hey!!). I mean, if he's so dumb that he can't work out how to spend his retirement fund, then he must be seriously stupid too. My dad says that if Mr Nudes (that's what he calls him out of respect) hasn't got enough imagination to spend a quarter of a million dollars then he shouldn't be teaching kids. Anyway, that's what my dad says.

Besides, who would want to be a teacher and have kids like Joel cracking up in your class all the time? It's all right for me because Joel's my mate but I wouldn't want to be an old teacher and have to teach him. Not for anything. Teaching kids these days, what with drugs and violence and stuff, must be terrible.

My mum agrees with my dad. She says it's tragic but I'm not sure if she means being an old sick teacher is tragic or what Joel does to Nudes is tragic or just being Mr Nudes himself or even the problem of his big lump — well, lumps — if you follow me.

Joel isn't always bad. He gets on really well with our drama teacher, Miss Scarlett. Groovy name, hey? Miss Scarlett is really nice. She looks great too. Well, "interesting" as mum puts it. "Different," Dad says.

Miss Scarlett is what we call a Gothic over here. She wears really white make up. It looks a bit like plaster of Paris (get the French Connection). She's got long black hair and always wears long black clothes but she is kind of pretty. She looks a bit like Mortisha, you know the mum in the Adams Family? Pretty weird, but pretty. Anyway, she lets Joel get away with blue murder. He would do anything for her too. He does drama improvizations that really crack us all up. He wants to be a stand-up comedian like Seinfeld in a nightclub.

Miss Scarlett is strict and fair. That is what good teachers should be. Strict and Fair. The only time she really cracked up at Joel was when he started doing this impersonation of Mr Nudes. He put these two apples in this old pair of tights and gaffer-taped it to his leg, like down his jeans. (Joel doesn't wear school uniform because he bought a forged note in Year 8 saying he was allergic to the material.) Anyway then he came out the front of the class and jiggled the apples in the tights around. Did Miss Scarlett crack!! Like nuclear. She said it was the cruellest thing she had ever seen a student do. Joel really hated being called a student because he is wrapped in Miss Scarlett and really wants to be a man to impress her.

But she was right. I mean, Nudes isn't funny. He is sad. Anyway, Joel is feeling pretty good right now because he gets his Learner's Permit to drive in a week. Then he reckons he's going to shoot through.

Speaking (writing) of shooting through, isn't it about time you told me how come you ran away from home? I mean, you embarrassed me when you wrote "With Affection" at the end of your letter, then you didn't tell me anything special at all except about being in love. If you can tell me that (even if he is a geeky Italian waiter), how come you still haven't 'fessed up about your Dad? You know, keeping things like that inside is not good for you. It's like having a big pimple on your mind, kind of. That's what friends are for, hey, to help you squeeze it. To talk out your problems. Besides, who am I going to tell your problems to if I am a million ks away over here? It's not like you're Madonna and the whole world is listening with battered breath for the hot goss about you. And besides I told you about Joel's problems and my sister Teresa (the closet bed-wetter) and some other personal stuff, so ...

Anyway, I am sorry to hear that France isn't so good with brass bands. I really hate brass bands. My grandfather likes brass bands. He lives in a nursing home and wanders away unless the nurses keep an eye on him. He is too much for mum and dad to mind. But he is a nice old bloke and likes talking about the 1950s in Springvale when it used to be all dairy farms before it got subdivided for houses and a tip. Anyway, Grandpa likes brass bands and he has got old records that he plays, all tooting and farting and booming, and all the other oldies in the home have to listen because he plays them at recreation hour when everyone sits in the sun room. We try not to visit then.

I don't think that I want to grow old. I would rather get hit by a truck when I am seventy and go out quick, but my mum says I shouldn't think like that because its tempting fate. That's my mum. Always watching out for omens.

So, hear from you soon. Hope your heart doesn't get broken.

Lotsa luv

Venny the Photogenius One

Letter 8

Ashok Hotel
50-B Chanakyapuri
New Delhi 110.021
India

September 15

Dear Venny

It's been so-o-o-o long. And this time I'm truly sorry about time going and going — maybe 5 months? We've been here — it must be 3 months now. Not at this hotel all the time, but for lots of it. I know I last wrote you when I was in Cannes — and when I was in love (was, note well) and when I was looking forward to going to the French countryside to a groovy château that Aunt Bea had told me all about. (Friend of a friend's castle kind of deal.)

Well, that didn't happen, the bellhop dumped me and then my tutor turned up. For a while there I'd thought I might escape Bypass Kev altogether! It turned out that my boyfriend Carlo was after one thing and he cooled off big time almost the minute he got it. I couldn't really believe it but after a big romantic time with him, he dropped me just like that! I'm sitting waiting at the breakfast table one morning just to exchange passionate glances like we were doing all week, and he comes by with this French chick who was moving into the hotel

51

with her Dad. And is he all eyes for her or what? I was so indignant I left the table and bumped into him in front of the lifts. He had the grace to blush, but not the guts to say anything. And then I saw him leaving the hotel with her that afternoon — by our usual exit! He didn't have anything to say about that either — but I did! He gave me back all my love-notes the next day. So much for Latin lovers! (Big joke.) I've vowed never to fall in love like that again! Never. Ever. (No joke.)

Aunt Bea obviously had a bee in her bonnet in Cannes. She was too distracted to notice my red eyes and the fact that I was mooching round the hotel absolutely heart-broken. She met with another big-time movie director here (I know because the maid in the hotel told me, she was so impressed). But Aunt Bea came home all dispirited after one meeting with him. And I overheard a bit of a phone conversation later about her mysterious purpose here: "He's moved on again and I simply have to talk to him, even if it means going to the ends of the earth!" Which we have done!

Look, I know she's on the trail of somebody. Or something! Maybe she had a secret son or daughter. Or maybe it's a murder trail? God knows. You probably think I should just ask her outright, but you don't know Beatrice. You just can't enter into her private business. She's got this kind of icy wall around her when it comes to personal matters. And she's autocratic, which means she calls the shots.

So, without explanation, we've moved on. After a few frantic days of faxes and emails and phone calls, Bea simply announced a major change of plan. Now we've made a beeline (hah) for India — exotic, amazing, riveting maybe — but not what I was expecting at all.

Here I was, looking forward to horses and dogs (I'm still missing Spaghetti so much!). Here I was, expecting French countryside with black-and-white cows in the meadows, and we get over-crowded, multi-polluted New Delhi. We get traffic, including cows, along with trucks and taxis and sedans and auto-rickshaws — and people like you could never believe! People everywhere — the sheer impact of millions living on the streets all around you. There are these crazy tin sheds in the outlying parts that are shops selling wares, sari lengths, bangles, bamboo ladders — you name it! Even things like tooth extractions (with everyone watching).

I love it here, the hustle and bustle, but honest to God it's like going to war the first few times you go out into the street. Merchants and hawkers make a beeline for you (to use that word again). And you've got to get tough real quick.

The first time they crowded in around me with some very pretty little souvenir replicas of the Taj and God knows what, and I hummed and haa'd because they were so cheap. I was a goner. Meaning droves of others came around to sell their wares and I couldn't get away. Then, after I did, the beggars came after me — and there are lots of them hanging just off-camera all around the posh hotels. You can't blame them and I feel sorry for them, but they also drive you MAD! Sometimes they can be frightening, pressing in around you and shouting, "Madam Madam, me, me!" like they're desperate — and you know they really are.

Aunt Bea said I shouldn't give them anything. "Only encourages them." She makes it a policy not to give, as she has her charities at home. Some of her money goes to India, she says. (That's true, I'm sure, but — hell — people looking you in the face like this!) According to her, the huge new middle class of India (yes, there are a lot of very rich and moderately rich people here) ought to be doing more for the poor (which is true again, but ...).

Whatever she says, I secretly keep a swatch of small notes to give to kids when they come up to me. Some of them are cheeky, mind you, and ask for another and another, but lots of them are pitiful. You soon realize that the problem is never-ending here. But you can't turn off your feelings about people fending for themselves on the street — especially the little kids. And I don't think you should, even though the guides often like to give you the line that many of the beggars are secret millionaires. Oh, sure!

Aunt Bea decided I should "experience" India — that is, see the countryside and the people — on our way to visit the Taj Mahal. As if you don't see enough of everyone every time you go onto the streets of Delhi!

Going by rail to Agra meant getting up at 5 am. Just crossing the railway bridge almost broke my heart. Not only skinny-as-hell dogs sleeping there but the real poor of the city. Old men and women — or maybe they weren't so old — kids, grandmothers, whole families, sleeping on newspaper spread on the floor. And "rags" doesn't describe what some of them were wearing.

Lots of families were still fast asleep in clumps all over the station itself. Then I saw a man coming along

54

with a stick to prod them awake as the sun rose. He wasn't awful, just gently wakening them, but obviously they had to get off the station in the daytime. Watching people yawning and stretching, I couldn't help thinking, What if that was me there? What kind of day are they looking forward to? What kind of breakfast, for that matter?

Only half the kids go to school here, so there are lots who never learn to read and write. I mean I've heard all this before, but somehow when you're right here and there's a girl about your own age, face to face, someone with lustrous eyes who you know doesn't have a chance in the world — you begin to think about a lot of things.

Like, in my case, how I've ended up living in the lap of luxury, even though I started out in a trailer park with dysfunctional parents (as described by my shrink and echoed enthusiastically by Aunt Beatrice). It's a country that makes you laugh and cry on the same day, in the same hour, and it sure as hell makes you think.

Everything in India seems bittersweet. The Taj Mahal is the BIG Indian cliché, I suppose, but when you see it for real, it just knocks your socks off. It's exhilarating. (By the way, you have to take off your shoes to go inside the Taj Mahal when you go to view the coffin. Did I say it's a tomb?)

And guess what, in the garden which leads up to the Taj, I sat on Princess Diana's seat. There's a famous photo of her looking lovelorn in front of the Taj. (Isn't "lovelorn" a beautiful word?) She was obviously just staring at the great edifice that was built for love. The seat was in the garden, which has a long pond, or more a channel, with fountains leading up to the marble stairs. In case you don't know, the Taj Mahal is a MONUMENT TO LOVE. A maharaja called Shah Jahan built it for his wife, Mumatz Mahal. She died giving birth to a baby girl — her 14th kid — on June 7th, 1631, the guide book says. (That happens to be my birthday!)

The maharaja was away fighting some war or other and she was in a tent behind the lines, because they couldn't bear to be apart, not even for a few weeks. He was devastated by her death and he didn't eat or speak to anyone for a week afterwards.

Shah Jahan was so lovelorn, so frantic without Mumatz, he sent his kingdom into severe mourning for two years and then came up with the idea of building a tomb to her memory, the most exquisite of its kind in the world. The guide book says it took 22 years to build and 22 thousand people worked on it. It had real gold and real silver, sheets of real pearls, pounds of real emeralds and other precious stones set in the walls and — here's something for the world atlas — crystal from China, lapis lazuli from Sri Lanka, agate from Yemen, coral from the Red Sea and turquoise from Tibet, to tell you only a teeny-tiny bit. Impressed? You would be if you saw it! The place is too-oo beautiful to describe.

When we first caught sight of it Aunt Beatrice said, "Remember this moment. We're gazing on beauty, Saffron. Beauty!" She had tears in her eyes. I knew she was right and I was glad Bypass was way behind us, still coming through the men's security gate.

What a place, and what a love story! I wonder if anyone will ever want to do something extravagant for me? Not that I want a tomb just yet, but you know ... a grand gesture, even a smallish grand gesture!

That's not the end of the story either. The maharaja's own son eventually imprisoned his father in the Red Fort, another colossal building across the river from the Taj. Every morning he would look out of the royal apartment (which was gorgeous but still a prison) at the Taj where his beloved lay. But he never visited it again! He died in the Red Fort. I know I'm going on and on, but we've just come back from there and my mind is whirling with thoughts of white marble, precious gems and love.

I have thought about you in the past few months, but I couldn't find your last letter and didn't like to write you without at least reminding myself of what you said. And today I found it in my diary. So Mr Nudes aside (your lumpy teacher sounds pretty sad, like you said), I thought about your friend Joel. I remember them trying to put that ADD label on me once, which was crazy for me because I'm the opposite. Kind of obsessed by things and too focused.

Anyway, I feel sorry for Joel because another kid at school had the same thing and she couldn't really learn anything. But I don't feel sorry that he was bawled out by Miss Scarlett doing that impersonation. I mean it sounded funny and I bet it raised a laugh or three. But I have a problem with things like that.

You see, my mother was fat. And I mean real fat, so that it was like an affliction, I suppose. And I remember some kids stuffing cushions down their backs and fronts and so on at the Trailer Park Christmas Concert where she was singing, and taking her off. And it was awful. I'll never forget her face that night. All vulnerable and with this stupid fixed smile as everyone round us broke up with that impersonation of her. I'll never forget it — she was smiling but I knew it felt like there was an ice pick in her heart. Her mouth was all wobbly with that cheesy grin she used to get when she felt real bad. You've got to judge sometimes what a laugh is actually worth, don't you think?

Mom went home that night and raged and cried. And then got absolutely hammered and cried some more and we had a miserable Christmas. The worst.

I thought I told you something very special in my letter, even though you said I didn't. I mean, what's more special than being in love? And about my Dad — I don't talk about him much, not even in my diary, so maybe one day — I don't know. And about my shrink — I'll tell you all about him sometime, but not now, Venny.

We're about to move on to Chennai, where there is a place called "Bollywood." Honest to God. And surprise, surprise, that's where they make the Indian movies by the thousands. When you look at Indian television it's a hoot. I mean, I'm romantic, but the stories are way over the top! The actors break into song at the craziest moments and there's lots of gazing adorably and adoringly into each other's eyes. It's a far cry from Hollywood, let me tell you. I don't think they're allowed to show anything more sexual than a kiss, so there's lots of other foreplay stuff but never, never the real thing!

So, Bollywood, here we come, and I hope to hell the person Aunt Beatrice is looking for is hanging out there. Because some of the film stars, even though their films are pretty crappy, are hot! Maybe I'll get to meet one or two. I fancy I'll be able to get a lot more info. about this diversion to India from Bypass. He has a drinky-poo in the evening and sometimes he gets very talkative. I'm biding my time. ("Biding" is a good word too, isn't it?)

I just want to go hang out in the countryside. You might be getting the message I like animals. Well, I do, but Aunt Bea promised me painting lessons when we settle a little, and big city hotels are not the place. I've got this feeling about doing a great big painting and I know just what I want to do — it's kind of abstract but not absolutely. Anyway, Chennai is just another big city and it won't be the place to get a great big roll of canvas.

Bea reckons we're going to stay in the Lake Palace on the way back from Chennai, so that sounds groovy, and at least I'll be able to swim. It's built in the middle of the lake, no less, and one of the maharaja's families once owned it or probably still does, and the royal family of England stays there! So why not us?

Funny thing, Venny, I thought I was broken-hearted in Cannes. There's something to be said for moving on or moving around. I remember in old English novels that wayward sons or daughters were always taken "abroad" to Europe for months on end to get over their forbidden loves. It seems to work! Since getting here I'm almost completely distracted. There's so much to see and do (including lots of homework from Kev, unfortunately), and Carlo has receded already. I admit to keeping his first love letter, though, and I still read it sometimes when I'm feeling blue. It was so charming, the way he had of saying things about his feelings, and it had lots of misspellings like yours. And I thought it was heartfelt! Oh well.

Please write me care of the Ashok Hotel address above — they'll forward our mail. I'm really looking forward to hearing from you, and my mind is clearer now, I think. Post Cannes and post Carlo!

You were so cute about that "with affection" stuff, but it's true I do feel affection for this not altogether unknown boy across the water, i.e. YOU! And not so far away now either (time difference of only 4½ hours from Australia — you're ahead). I'd like to know more about your life. Write me.

Would just plain "with love" be better? Anyway, here goes.

With love

Saffron

Letter 9

27 September

Dear Saffron

You sure made me wait a long time for your letter. I was nearly going to write to you twice in a row because I have got a lot to fill you in on – like how I landed a job as a photographic model! Honest! But first of all I guess I have to be polite and reply to all the stuff you told me.

Well, you can't say I didn't warn you about that Italian waiter. I mean I'm real sorry that he hurt you and everything, but I saw this show on TV once that warned guys that if they wear tight underwear to bed (like tight jocks and not boxer shorts) it stirs up their testosterone levels and they get really randy. I hope you don't think I'm trying to come on to you or anything by saying that, but since you haven't got a dad around I guess its up to me to tell you. I don't reckon your Aunty B would be much help, so if ever you want to know anything about guys, just ask, OK? So I'm saying your Carlo was probably over-sexed because he was wearing those tight waiters pants all day. Anyway, I thought I had better tell you that since it might make you feel a bit better seeing the problem from his point of view, you know?

India sounds pretty interesting but remember that I'm not really into other countries. Not that what you wrote was boring, but don't overdo it, especially with the descriptions. There was also a fair bit of "love talk" in your letter too, and I'm not into that either. The part about the Taj Mahal was cool but I think it probably means more to you than it does to me. I hope that when (if?) I fall in love it works out for me — like my girlfriend doesn't die or anything, you know. I wrote "my girlfriend" because I guess I will fall in love with a girl since I'm not gay (so far as I know). Still, you have to keep an open mind about these things, don't you? I mean, like my mum always says, "You never know what's around the corner, Venny."

Another funny thing about your letter — not funny ha-ha — funny queer (oops, gay word!) is that you saw beggars just when I was making one. I told you yonks ago I really get off on making built sculpture in art like that jaguar I sent you the photo of. I really like creating (hey, this dude is "so sophisticated!!") skinny, slinky things that show muscles and sinews under the skin, so I made this figure of a beggar. Coincidence, hey, but I didn't tell mum because she would say it was fate that what you were seeing I was making, and "something would come of it."

I made the beggar's head out of a metal Star Wars figure that I rubbed back and polished to look like a skull (It was C3PO the droid so I didn't have much to do there.) His body was made by spot welding really thin chain links that I turned up in the rubbish tip. I like the sculpture a lot because the metal makes the beggar look really stark and cold and the links make him look hollow. Both of those things suit a beggar. It is a seated fig-

62

ure about 80 cm high so it makes a statement. I soldered an empty sardine tin in his hand because I reckon you would really have to be starving to eat sardines.

Anyway, if you do write more about India, tell me about the people like snake charmers. I saw this picture once in a magazine that showed an Indian holy man with his head stuck in a hole. (Funny that!) This guy looked like an ostrich. The magazine said that he didn't suffocate because he was able to lower his pulse and breathing rate like a hibernating animal. I am really into weird stuff like snake charmers and psychic healers and mystical powers, and India is really cool like that. If I was born when my parents were (like two hundred years ago) then I might have been a hippy and gotten into transessential meditation. That's a form of therapy Joel's counsellor is trying on him to help him calm down, but Joel reckons that all he sees are visions of girls in see-through clothes (maybe that's what transessential really means?) like those cheesecloth dresses hippy chicks used to wear. I never know for sure when Joel is lying but he always makes me laugh.

Anyway, I said that I would tell you about how I got this excellent job. Well, I went to the Year Ten Formal last July (that's how long it is since you wrote to me). I guess you would call the Formal the Prom, like American movies are always having this mass murder on Prom night (as if!). Anyway I wasn't going to go since only the up-themselves dudes go with their sucky prefect girlfriends, but then this major babe called Gayle Warning (honest to God that's her real name) came over to me one recess and asked me to go with her. I was eating this sloppy pie and upchucked all down the front of my school uniform I got such a surprise. Gayle Warning is a part-time model. Honest, she is a babe. I mean like a Nicole Kidman babe, but not stuck up. She's tall (but not as tall as me) and "willowy" (which is how my fat little sister Teresa describes her) and blonde.

Anyway, I have included a couple of photos —one of us both on the night dressed up in our good gear. I had to hire a dinner suit. (I am the one in the dinner suit.) And yes, the pants were tight as hell, so I got to prove that TV theory and it wasn't funny!! You will see that we are standing beside the bar at the Springvale Taverna and Function Centre where the Formal was held, but we weren't allowed to drink being under age (yeah sure). But the main thing is you can see what Gayle looks like.

She didn't really spend much time with me that night. Her father picked me up from home and dropped us off in his Jag and then after we arrived and the photos got taken she dumped me and hung around with her girlfriends. I hung around near the punch bowl all night. It was bad.

This particular photo was published in the Springvale News (which is a rag) and then because Gayle is a model it got syndicated in the "Gold Coast Times" (which is like a mega circulation to all the rich doods who live in condos on the coast) and then a couple of days after that I heard this weird announcement when I was in Science saying, "Venero Merlo, Venero Merlo, report to administration immediately. Venero

Merlo, report to administration immediately. Phone call, Venero Merlo." I thought that Grandpa was dead for sure, because they only call students to Admin. when someone has died, so I was nearly crying when the receptionist told me to pick up the phone and this really deep voice said, "Venero, this is Anthony van der Fleete from Catwalk magazine. Could your teacher spare you a moment?"

I thought jeez, this guy must want his car greased or something, and I said, "Yeah what can I do ya for?" Then he says, "You are the Venero Merlo who accompanied Gayle Warning to the Springvale High Formal, aren't you?" I told him I was and then he asked me if I knew that Gayle was a model. I said, yes, I'd heard the rumour but I didn't believe it. Then he says, "I'm calling you on Gayle's recommendation and after seeing your photograph with her in the 'Gold Coast Times,' we were wondering if you could come down for a photo shoot?"

I thought this must have been a set-up Joel had organised and started joking around, but then I worked out that this guy was serious so I scribbled down the address and got my dad to run me over to the agency after school. I just wore my jeans and a T-shirt although I got Teresa to put gel in my hair and wore dad's aftershave and that sort of thing.

This Anthony guy was there and he took me into a studio and had me stand and sit around while this photographer took like thousands of photos. They didn't ask me to take my shirt off or anything, so that was good, and after a while I started to relax. The photographer was an

OK young guy and set up lights and stools and benches for me to lean or sit on and told me how to "pose" (tilt your head, shoulders back, more to your left, etc).

They didn't say much at the time and then two days later I got this phone call at home to ask me if I would come down and see the "folio" which they said was "brilliant" and "commercial." I got the bus over. The photos didn't really look much like me but they looked pretty professional — all glossy in black and white. Maybe I'll send you one of them next time, just for a laugh.

Next thing Anthony asked me if I would do some more for a client who was advertising a new line of jeans imported from Italy and I was the "perfect model" for them. He said I would get paid $200 for every photo that the client picked, but Anthony's agency would get a cut of 25%. So that's how I got this modelling job. It's great. I am making like $300 a month and sometimes I get to keep the clothes as well.

A couple of my mates have really bagged me (saying I'm a poofter which means gay in Oz) but I don't take any notice. I'm making really good money and learning heaps. I get to meet people at the studio and a couple of times I've been to parties Anthony puts on down there for his clients and fashion buyers. There are people from all over the world at these dos, even a buyer from Cannes. I told her about you and how you had been there so it was good to sound like I knew something about the place. It also means that I have to watch how I speak and not sound like a total moron Year 11 kid from Springvale High School. I see a fair bit of Gayle at these dos. She says "Hi" but we aren't going together or anything. (Even if I wanted a girl-friend I wouldn't have time for one now.) Gayle told me its a good idea to just stand there and listen and learn, but I reckon these people accept me for what I am most of the time. Only one or two fashion design-ers have tried to "put on the dog" and ignore me or talk down to me.

Anthony says that my greatest asset is my height. I'm 6 foot 1" (185 cm) now. He also says I have good bone structure (cheek bones). Gayle wants to use her model-ling experience to get into acting and says that I should try to do the same, so I'm trying to take my Speech and Drama lessons more seriously, though it's not easy with Joel cracking me up every five minutes.

It's pretty hard to tell him and some of my other mates that I can't hang around with them as much as I used to because of my work. Joel's got his driver's li-cence now and I have a learner's permit, but I never have time to take lessons so I might never get my li-cence, which mum says is just as well. Joel's got this 1978 Ford Falcon which my dad (who is a panel-beat-er) keeps patching up as bits fall off like the exhaust. (Joel really liked having no exhaust to tell you the truth.) He is a bit of a hoon. Anyway, the way things are going, if I save my money I should be able to get a decent car. I would like something smooth — a European car like an old BMW or an Alfa and then I would have to get a licence.

So that's the way things are shaping up over here. The future is looking pretty good but my mum says that I'm tempting fate if I say that. Anyway, I hope you like the photos. I think that I'm not such a big jerk as I used to be anymore.

With lots of love

Venero

PS. The other photo I put in was one Joel took of me outside Dad's shed in our back yard. Notice that I'm holding your last letter — just to prove I got it!

Letter 10

4 November

Dear Saffron

I haven't heard from you so I was worried that my last letter might have made you cranky at me. You know, with all the stuff about modelling you might think that I'm showing off. A smart-arse, as they say over here. Or I thought that maybe something happened to you. Like you might have met someone and fallen in love again and don't want to write to me anymore or maybe you've had an accident or caught a disease in India. I won't say any more in case you have got either one (boyfriend or disease).

So, will you do me a big favour? If you can't write (or don't want to write any more), will you just write me one last letter? You know, to tell me why? That might sound weird because I hardly know you, but I think we could be really good mates — well, friends, anyway. Different sides of the tracks, you know? I'm saying, I hope you still want to write. And please write a little letter even if you don't. OK?

I'm a bit scared of telling you any more about my life in case I upset you, but since I'm in my computer class and have got time, I will. I want to anyway, but you know what I said before.

So — the modelling thing has really taken off for me. I'm getting so much work I can't hardly keep up.

All these other agencies are asking for my folio so I am being syndicated, as they call it. My boss, Tony van der Fleete, says it's OK if I syndicate because the more exposure I get (photo-wise, I mean), the better it is for my career and for him so long as I stay on his books. Just to make sure I do stay with him he has offered me a contract. Cool. I don't want to get a big head about it, but it means I get regular money which is great.

I have had to buff up a bit though. I mean, go to the gym and work out. I had to buy bike pants because that's what they wear at the gym. Pretty embarrassing. I've been working out for a few months now and I can see a big difference. Like I'm not in my old body any more. Now I've got pecs and abs (not real big but they're there) and that sort of stuff that you read about in muscle magazines. I don't want to be a testosterone muscle man though. Like some people have to study because their brain is their meal ticket, I have to work out because my body is my meal ticket. That's what Tony tells me. Scary, hey? So going down to the gym is like studying or doing homework. But alright! See, I'm thinking that I might try making modelling my real job. Like a career. It might lead to movies which would be totally excellent. (More babes — I wish!)

Sure, there's some cute girls at the gym so it's fun most days. They are all pretty nice to me. I've been out with a couple (OK, OK, in a group) but I haven't done anything. (So I'm still a virgin.) They all put on the dog, which doesn't impress me a lot.

My mate Joel has settled down a bit in school (new medication) which is a good thing but he's still crazy in his car. A real hoon. He's shaved his head and got a nose ring. And he got one somewhere else too, he reckons. Fowl. He's got a tatt on his arm too. It says wild thing and shows a creature like a Tasmanian Devil showing its fangs. He's a bad, bad, boy, Joel is. He's had sex a million times in the back of his car (V8 Ford Falcon, rust bucket) at the drive-in movies with a million different girls. He likes the rough ones. But I still really like him.

Anyway, I hope that you get this and write back. I miss your letters. Write soon even if you're not going to write any more. I am still me, you know. Like I'm not famous or anything. Well, not yet, hey?

Venero

Letter 11

Waldorf Astoria Hotel
301 Park Avenue
New York NY 10022-6897

November 19

Dear Venero

It's so strange I got your letter today because I've been thinking of you for the last few days. Honest to God! And I'm sorry I didn't answer the one before that. We've been on the move and, to tell the truth, I've been kept rather busy coping with my aunt, who has been difficult. (Reversal of roles you might say, but I do think she's been acting very childish — certainly extravagant — but more of her later.)

Yes, I received your other letter with the groovy news that you are now making a career of modelling. How cute! That's real good for you, Venero. I can sense it because the whole feeling of your letters has changed. If I were a shrink I'd say that your sense of self has developed lots — and your self-esteem and confidence. How's that? You can tell the story of your "discovery" when you become a super-model like the ones they interview on "Oprah" or "Good Morning America" or whatever!

If you *do* go down the modelling path, though, just don't get too in love with yourself, that's all I want to say! I knew this girl in New York in my brief time at school there and she became so totally engrossed in her body that she was a bore. She talked about diet and muscle tone ad nauseum and she carried her make-up to bed with her, we all maintained. She wouldn't do sports with us in case she got a tan that was uneven! She had to work out every day and she had a passion for ice cream. If she ate one ice cream she told us she had to skateboard ten miles to deal with the fat content (which she knew to the last half-ounce) because she did shoots about fat-free foods! She always seemed to be punishing herself and then talking about it endlessly.

Joel does sound pretty wild to me, but he's probably exaggerating that stuff about all those girls. Lots of boys do and you should know that. But I'd like to ask you why you're still a virgin? Seems strange to me if you are out in the modelling world the way you say you are. You're not frightened are you, or gay or something? You do talk about your body a lot — and other people's — so I was just wondering. I don't mind either way, just curious.

And yes, I also read the bit about your model of a beggar. Was it synchronicity or what? (You can look that up — I'm not going to explain!) Because I'm painting again now and that scene on the railway station stayed in my mind. I did this kind of abstract painting about beggars. Amazing or what?

I won't bore you with more involved Indian tales,

except to say I saw a snake charmer and he wanted to wrap a python around my waist. As if! I had to pay him many rupees NOT to do it and Aunt Bea said that, as usual, I was taken in and it was a trick. But would you like to have a python shoved up your sweater, so to speak? Not that you wear a sweater in India!

We went to Rajasthan to stay at the Lake Palace as planned, and wow! You travel by boat to this marble palace and I can tell you it was exactly like being in a fairy-tale. It was night time and we went sort of gliding over this dark water, pushing through hyacinths that grow in clumps at the landing jetties. All the time my eyes were on this delicate, white, wedding-cake palace sitting in the middle of the lake. Talk about gorgeous! And so was the bellhop who helped us to the suite. (Aunt Bea only ever stays in a suite, you know, which suits me as I wouldn't want to share a room with her — she's on the phone endlessly.) But I guess I'm still licking my wounds over Carlo and Cannes, and I just gave this guy a very cool stare and made sure Aunt Bea did the tipping.

Every morning I went down to the pool, which was in a James Bond movie ages ago but they are still talking about it, and it was probably the biggest thing that happened here since the maharana (posher and more powerful than a mere maharaja) had his harem of 500 gals come on holidays here. I set up my easel and painted. This is because my friend, companion and tutor, Mr Bypass, has kind of bypassed me again. (Sad to say we are to be reunited.)

74

Look, it's too long to go into detail about what's happening and I'm not absolutely sure, as I told you, but we hung out round Bollywood for a while and Aunt Beatrice met up with this actor guy, Feisal Chander. Feisal is charming as, but I think he's led her on a wild-goose chase. One day in her room I saw money from the pigskin briefcase exchanging hands — lots of it. He kept on saying, "We're getting close, Ms Duval, for sure! Have patience, Ms Duval." Any rate, he had her on the run-around to places outside Chennai just about every few days. She insisted on taking me on these trips to nowhere to meet no one, and when we came home she was so agitated I had to stick around. So what with Bypass and lessons and then wild-goose chases to places like this ashram in Pondicherry, which was very pretty, but where we waited for a person who didn't show, once again, I've had no time to write.

The thing is she came back from one of those trips and told me we had to go home again.

"Already?" I asked her, because she'd promised we'd go round the world.

"For a short time," she said in that tone of voice. But we didn't go home at all. We're in New York, yes, but not in our apartment on Park Avenue. We're in the Waldorf Astoria on the 17th floor in — you guessed it — a suite! And I'm not to let anyone know that I'm back. Make what you will of it, we're sort of holed up in luxury. (It's only the second day and since I can't go out too much, I have lots of time to write you.)

I made up my mind I'd ask her point blank what in the hell is going on, but she's so unreachable I just can't. Oh, Venny, I feel so lonely and locked up sometimes, even in India in the wide open spaces, because I sense her tension and sadness all the time. I'm the one who has to have the patience, but right now I feel like I'm running out of it. She napped this afternoon and I got out to do some skating in Central Park. That will keep me going for a while. But tomorrow I'm going to ask her what the hell this running around is all about — I really am. Don't you think I have a right to know?

I missed you too, and I promise I won't leave it so long next time. I'm glad you sound so happy.

Love

Sapphron

(The real spelling of my name, since you've gone formal with Venero)

PS. It's funny, but I must admit to feeling just a bit jealous about that Gayle girl. You two standing there together look very much like a couple, and why I should care I'm sure I don't know. But it gave me a pang, you might say. You look very grown up and quite sexy in those pictures, I have to say!

I hope you like the photo I'm enclosing of me by the pool in the Lake Palace. Isn't it pretty (the pool, I mean)? I'm not fishing or anything, but I thought maybe I shouldn't send any more photos now that you're a fully fledged model going out with fully fledged models, with a professional folio of photos! But then I thought, what the hell!

PPS. Thanksgiving is coming up soon. I just wonder where this little family will be — Aunt Bea and me, that is.

Letter 12

Dear Sapphron

Calling you that sounds weird, but it sounds sophisticated too so I'll try it. I'm really into sophisticated at the moment. Cool, hey?

After I got your last letter I felt pretty awful. Here I was raving on about myself and you were way over there in trouble. I think I sort of knew that in my heart but I thought it was a guy or that you were sick. To tell you the truth, the guy thing worried me the most, but it sounds like you can take care of yourself. Except for all this mystery about your Aunty Beetroot. Jeez, I couldn't stand it getting the run around like that. Is she crazy or what? Sounds to me like she's got so much money she doesn't know what to do with it. But it's not her I'm worried about. It's you.

It's good that you're starting to open up and tell me things. That's what friends are for, hey? And I'm the best sort of friend to tell because I don't know any of your friends or rellies so I can't go around dobbing on you. So feel free to use me to get it all out of your system. When you find out what's wrong, that is. I really mean that, Saf. (Oops, there goes Sapphron.) I mean that, honest. When you say you're lonely I can't help thinking about you.

You know it wasn't the pool I was looking at in that photo you sent. It was you and you don't need to worry about fishing for complements because I would have told you that you look great anyway. And going skating doesn't sound like the answer, even if it was in Central Park. So far as I know that's where they have big concerts and you need a friend to go with. Skates aren't much company. So, let me know.

Writing is good for you, I reckon. Phone calls just make you feel worse. You always want to ring back and say, "I meant to say ..." if you know what I mean. Writing is good because you can go back and change what you wrote or even throw it in the bin (like my English teachers always do, I bet). So work it all out on paper if you can and send it to me. I promise I will read it all. And even give you advice if you want. Like if I'm not a model or a panel beater, I could write a lonely hearts column.

That advice that you gave me turned out to be right. Modelling is weird, hey? Things change. Mum says that our lives are like the sands through the hourglass. Mum's like that.

Anyway, not long after I wrote to you I got this catwalk gig. It was my first and I was high as a kite. It was at this classy resort on the Gold Coast. Megabucks. I was booked to model this new range of Italian designer jeans that I told you about. OK, so I went to a few rehearsals which went pretty well but it's a lot different from just rolling up for a photo shoot. You have to know how to move to music and work with a team of other models. Like you warned me, I met a few real jerks. Really full of themselves, they were. After the first rehearsal one guy got me back in the change room and said that I walked in front of him on purpose to try to upstage him. Jeez, all I was worried about was not falling off this plank that you're supposed to walk on. Then these two female models — Shaleen and Oondala (that's their names. Honest. I just use my real name) — well, they lined me up and abused me for being too clumsy and having no rhythm. Hell. I don't want to be a disco dancer. Still, I know now why they call it catwalk modelling. The people can be pretty nasty.

Anyway, there's a good side. That first night this rep (Public Relations/Advertising) for the jeans company said that she would drive me home. I said sure. I still haven't got my licence (even though I turned 17 a couple of months ago) and I usually get a taxi. That costs a hell of a lot and really eats into my fee. Since this was only a rehearsal, the money was less anyway. The rep's name is Ros Daniels and she's really nice. She talked a lot about the industry and how she thought that I would go a long way. She said she had watched me and I had "It," whatever that means, but it sounded cool. When she dropped me off I felt great. She drives a black BMW Roadster. (Cool. Cool. Cool.)

Next rehearsal was better and I didn't stand on any toes. Afterwards Ros drove me home again (top down), only this time she asked me if I'd like a coffee at her favourite café. I was a bit worried because it was midnight and I still go to school (I don't say that too loud to the other models, especially the babes), but I said sure because I liked talking to her (especially about my future) and besides I didn't want to offend her. She's got her problems too. She just ended a five-year relationship with this big-time hero football star called Brad Jones and she said she's still hurting.

I don't know why she wants to tell me all this, but she must think I've got a sympathetic ear or something (see, I could write a lonely hearts column, hey?). She did say that putting time into developing my career would help get her mind off her troubles. She said that if I broke my contract with Tony van der Fleete she could do big things for me. I don't want to get Tony offside because he gave me my first break, but hey, you have to think of yourself sometimes too.

The actual gig went off really well and I didn't fall off the catwalk, so Ros took me out to a restaurant afterwards to celebrate. It was really great. She's very sophisticated and good-looking (but not really a babe — more of a woman). I feel like a million dollars when she takes my arm. Cool. I really like her and trust her and think that she will do a lot for me in the future.

Sorry to rave on about Ros and my career but that's what's on my mind at the moment.

Back to your letter. It was really weird how you said you were painting a beggar. (I didn't need to look up synchronicity either, by the way. Sync means together as in synchromesh gears in a car and chronos means time. I'm not a total moron, Miss Globe-Trotter.) Trouble is that with all that's going on in my life I haven't got time for my art stuff. In fact, it's a bit embarrassing to think that I even showed you that jaguar sculpture.

School is pretty hard to take these days. I go into my last year soon and I can hardly wait to get out. What we have to study is just crap compared to my real life. I mean, I used to want to pass so I could get a job as a panel beater like my dad, but all that's a thing of the past. More sands through the hourglass, hey? There's no way now that I'm modelling that I'm going to get covered in grease and paint. Besides, I don't want to work with all those yobbos in a panel shop. Not that I'm calling my dad a yobbo, if you know what I mean. Sure, I said that the other models can be bitchy but I don't have to end up like them, do I? When they are friendly they talk about adult things which my old friends like Joel don't.

I know that one time I told you I wasn't interested in travel but now I'm cut out of a lot of conversations because all the models talk about their travels or how much they want to work overseas. So I'm sorry I said that. Now I think of the great places you have been. Like the Taj Mahal and the Waldorf Astoria. I told Ros that I had a friend staying at the Waldorf Astoria and she went headless.

You know, when you first started writing to me (like 10 lifetimes ago), you said that you had "this maddening interest in words" (now you know I keep all your letters). Well, the same thing's happening to me. Last letter you wrote the word "Rajasthan." You know, Saff, reading about all the places you've been really turns me on now. I can really see them in my minds eye and I don't give a you-know-what when I go to the library and look in an atlas any more.

At least, if we get nuked, I'll know who dropped the bomb on me. Not like my mates who wouldn't even know where China was. Or Iraq (or the Waldorf Astoria). But it's not just the places you write about that get me in, it's the sound of their names. The sound of the actual word. I really like the letter "H" in Rajasthan. It makes you say "haan" which sounds so cool. Sophisticated. Like even Bollywood sounds like a tacky sort of Hollywood. I know that I can't live in Springvale and look out over the rubbish tip all my life. I have to grow up and get out. I want to see the world like you are. But not be lonely, like you. I would want go with a friend. Or even a lover, maybe? I wish!

Joel and my other old mates all make jokes about me now. They say I'm a poofter and gay because I do modelling. You can't be different from your mates in Australia. All they want to talk about is hotting up cars.

I often think about that boy Dwayne who was doing Home Economics. He copped heaps too, but now he's an apprentice chef in this really cool restaurant. In fact I saw him the night when Ros took me out to celebrate and he came over to our table. That's when I talked about the Waldorf Astoria. Dwayne's mouth dropped open too. I guess he had me figgered as a big jerk. But when he heard that and saw me with Ros I reckon he changed his mind. Dwayne's got a goal to be one of the world's greatest chefs. It's good that he's got a dream. And his hands and nails are clean and manicured. He's got a lot of class.

On the home front some things aren't so good. Mum and dad worry about me because I'm hardly ever home and when I am I'm late. Then there's mums' meals — she's always trying to "fatten me up" with all the pasta and stuff she makes. I have to watch my diet like you said your friend did, but there's a good reason for it. Too much food makes you sluggish and, well, fat. On Sundays she makes a a HUGE meal with pasta and roast meat and TONNES of side dishes and desserts to finish it off. And home-made breads on top of all that!

She's always done this but now she says she has to because on Sundays dad usually gets my grandpa out of the old peoples home. That's not only bad for me because I have to eat so much, but also it's really embarrassing because grandpa dribbles everywhere. Enough said. The school tuck shop (your "canteen?") only sells junk like pies and sausage rolls and cream buns. The cream isn't even real (not that I would eat it even if it was). And if I ask for sandwiches, the bread is always white. So it's hard ...

The only one who thinks my career is cool is my little sister. She's got all these photos of me on her wall next to Leonardo di Caprio and Brad Pitt. Very cool.

Yes, I am still a virgin. I wouldn't have admitted that once (and I still can't tell that to Joel and his mates) but I am. It's not that I'm getting all moral on you or anything. And no, I know I'm not gay either. Is it alright

84

for me to ask about you? I mean, have you ever done "it?" You don't have to tell me, but ...

So, that's how things are for me. I hope that when (if) you write back you tell me better news. And that you are feeling better. I guess it sounds silly but there are times when I think of you I would like to give you a hug. Models do that a lot. Not like my mates.

Please write and soon, and Merry Xmas and all that New Year stuff

Venero

PS. Another cool word that I now appreciate is "romantic." And no, it doesn't mean pashing and coming on and whatever. You use the word, but do you know what it really means? How about you look it up? You know, we are pretty synchronised, hey?

V.

Letter 13

Waldorf Astoria Hotel
301 Park Avenue
New York NY 10022-6897

20 December

Dear Venny

I wish you could see the streets of this little old town all lit up for Christmas, not to mention the foyer of this hotel. Then again, maybe one day you will!

Anyway, before I say anything at all about your last letter (which was fantastic!), I have to tell you about Beatrice and what she's admitted to me. We're still in the Waldorf Astoria, as you may have noticed from the letterhead, but in a few days we're heading out of here. The exciting news is that we're coming your way. No, not to Australia, but close! Somewhere up above you, to an island called Bali. So, no Spain or Italy, but a groovy part of the world I never thought I'd see. I'm imagining something like Hawaii — not that I've ever been there. Whatever, it'll be heaven to get away from this freezing cold. Any rate, maybe it's going to happen and we'll even get to meet! Can you get up to Bali, maybe?

Back to Beatrice. Yesterday I actually took courage and asked her who or what she's searching for. It'd been a strange day, one way and another, with lots of phone calls and mysterious appearances and disappearances.

Not with Mr Bypass, though. He's been on the job again, giving me morning lessons here in the hotel in his boring, boring way. But he's also actually been encouraging me to paint again, especially after he saw the sketches I did in France and the paintings from India. In fact he had Aunt Bea fix up this private room on the top floor where they store spare beds and junk in this place. They've cleared a space and put down drop sheets and, apart from the odd interruption of someone coming with my morning coffee (on a silver tray, what else?), it's a place where I can be alone. Heaven!

I overheard Kevin telling Aunt Beatrice that I had very real talent and he thought I was a "natural." She snorted at him in that imperious way of hers. "Of course she has — do you think I'd waste my time encouraging her otherwise? Why do you think I've taken the child travelling like this? To broaden her experience!" She didn't add, "You snivelling fool of a man," but it was there in her tone. However, it was Bypass, bless his unmatched socks and totally unfashionable boots, who got things organized for me in the end with an easel and paints and so on. (He's good for some things.)

I can't say I'm painting from nature like I want to, but I am painting from the life around me. The New York skyline is it at present. Have you seen the fab. pictures of this city by Georgia O'Keefe? (She's an American artist whose life reads like a movie.) Well, my pictures aren't exactly like hers, but let's say I'm working on them so that they will be mine. Like hers are hers! It's a funny thing, Venny, but when I see things in a certain clear way — like they're really shapes and colours and

87

beyond the mere thing I'm looking at — then I want to get the essence of the thing down on the paper or canvas right away. Like the Indian beggar wasn't just a beggar but an arrangement of lines and colour. Does that sound cold? I don't mean it to be, but somehow the shapes have to please me in every sense. In the colour sense and the line sense. And the texture sense. Does this make sense?

Back to Beatrice. She was talking to me rather than at me yesterday. For the first time. Said some almost kind things about my Mom. Said she understood why we were always on the move. (How could she? She wouldn't know a debt if she fell over one and broke her ankle on it!) But Aunt Beatrice and I had a heart to heart — well, for us.

What she didn't know was that I'd been down in the foyer, sitting near the bar and just kind of perving on the folks in all their glitz and minding my own business. Honestly! Suddenly this older man (30 at least) in a fab. suit and a gorgeous tie (I told him it was the best) came over and asked me if I'd like a drink, like I was fully grown up! I gulped a bit but then recovered myself enough to look real cool and just for fun I said, "Yes, why not?" When he got too talkative (he had two-and-a-half drinks to my one) I said unfortunately I had to go back up to my folks. You should have seen the look on his face when I said I was travelling with my aunt! I got in the elevator, waved him a fond goodbye with promises of coming back later, and hoped he wouldn't be there next time I came down through the foyer.

I was feeling a bit free and easy with the wine, I'd

have to say. I sucked a mint before I went back into our suite because I knew there'd be hell to pay if Beatrice guessed anything about drinking, let alone with a strange man. There she was, sitting at the window and sipping her Bourbon, and she spoke kind of soft and friendly for once. Because I felt the way I did, I just kind of blurted out all the things on my mind — all those burning questions.

Why did she stay and stay in places like Cannes and then just up and leave? And the same again in India? And where were we going next? And why couldn't we go home to our apartment, for God's sake? And just who was she looking for?

There was a long, long silence and I thought I'd really blown it. We were in the sitting room, which has the best view of the New York skyline, and I just fixated on the lights and waited. My heart was beating real fast. I can't explain how or why she makes me so nervous sometimes.

Anyway, at last she turned to me and said, "I'm going to tell you something, Saffron, and I hope that you can understand something of my problem." She had a very faraway look in her eyes and I didn't know if it was the drink or tears beginning.

She forged on. "There are some things which happen in your life that seem too hard to bear. They change you irreparably." (An ice pick in the heart again. I wanted to say, "As if I don't know that!" But she went on and her voice was edgy, so I said nothing.)

"The loss of my only son was one of them." She cleared her throat and poured some more booze, and I was pretty well struck dumb.

She'd never mentioned a son! Not to me or in her endless conversations with Françoise. The apartment where we live has no trace of any offspring. (I know, because I've been through the photo albums.) There is not one shred of evidence that a son has ever been any part of her life. Or her husband's.

"I'm searching for someone who knew him. It's as simple as that."

"But ... but ... " I had a dozen more questions on the tip of my tongue, I can tell you, and she knew it.

"That's all I want to say just now. When I find that person, then perhaps it will be time to explain more to you."

"But ... but ... " I know I sounded like a faulty CD or something.

"I'm seeking someone who can perhaps help me," she looked away into that polka-dot night, "perhaps ease the pain that his name has come to mean to me."

Then she sat up straight in the chair and sort of clicked back into her usual self. "At the moment that's all I'm prepared to say."

"Could I ask what his name was?" I spoke as gently as I could. I'm not that far away from the shock of the death of my Mom and I know about the pain that never, ever, leaves you, the deep part that doesn't bear thinking about too much. You can sometimes fool yourself it's being held at bay, but then it just presents itself — wham! — at a word from someone. Ice cold or red hot, whatever it is, it hurts like hell. Even if her son was long ago — after all, Aunt Bea is eighty-something — I didn't want to go blundering in on her feelings.

"Laurence." She spoke the name with such reverence

90

she could have added the word "Saint." My heart went out to her, but then she spoiled it by saying, "Poor Laurence," in a kind of — I don't know — a kind of condescending way.

"Could you tell me ... " I began again.

"That's it, Saffron." She picked up a magazine and flicked through some pages, pretending to see something that interested her and then reading intently.

There was another silence.

I just sat there, my mind racing. Why had she never mentioned a son? Where in the hell was he? She'd lost him. Was it an accident? A murder? I must admit I was kind of thrilled at the thought of this phantom son and the thought of a person somewhere who could reveal things even Beatrice didn't know. What kind of things? Was her son a dope addict? A dope dealer? My mind rushed to that end of the spectrum. Was her son somebody she was ashamed of? Maybe Beatrice and her husband had disowned him? And why did she want to find out things about him now, at the end of her life? He'd have to be about sixty if he'd lived. Had he died at forty, or thirty, or even twenty?

"I'll call for some tea," Bea murmured eventually and picked up the phone. I was so lost in thought I gave her the Beatrice treatment by not answering.

"And Saffron, my dear, the reason we can't go back to our apartment is because, apart from Françoise being there, I prefer it not to be known that I'm in town."

I was frowning and I knew she thought I was sulking, because she added something that surprised me.

91

"Look, Saffron, I don't want to sound dramatic and there's nothing untoward in this. Nothing at all. It's a missing persons matter and that's all."

"Mmm." I figured if I made no comment she would go on, and she did.

"I've had a private detective working on this thing for years. I'm now doing some detecting of my own without his knowledge. It's better this way. There were a few people in town this week who might have been able to help me. They're actors in a certain stage show. When we were in Pondicherry I learned that they had arrived in New York. I'm not going into that, because I don't think you should be troubled. Except to say this: they couldn't help me. Not even when I saw them face to face. So I must go on in my search for at least a while longer. We must go on. You want to accompany me, I assume? I'd like it if you would."

This was the first time she'd ever sounded anywhere near anxious for my opinion or my company.

"Of course I want to, Aunt!" I assured her.

"You might as well know we're following a sailor." She smiled for the first time. "And he's a fantastic voyager, as you might have guessed. But we should be home in time for you to sit your entry exams and take up your place at college in July. In case you're wondering."

My spirits drooped, because there's no way I meant to go to the college she'd planned for me. I have another plan altogether, but more about that later.

So now I'm a bit closer to the truth of our travels. And a bit closer to her. But whether I'll ever get the full story, who knows? Let's say I'm on red alert.

92

Venny, you're absolutely spot on about writing. I must admit that while I had that long, long gap in writing you, I was forever writing in my diary. I like rereading and rethinking. And sometimes it just seems to help control the chaos that is my life. Putting things down in black and white kind of cools your rage or angst, if you know what I mean.

Sometimes I write weird or funny things, and I wonder how in the hell I was in that kind of mood when I turn back to those pages. Pages of your life, hey?

I'm glad about your modelling career, Venny — it's changed you. I mean you still sound the same crazy person but, I'd have to say, not so much of a kid any more. In fact, when I think about it, and when I reread your letters (yes, I keep all of yours too), you sound way more grown up lately. And who's this Ros chick? You seem really keen and that's great. I think you should make a move if you really like her. Don't hang about. Life can just pass you by ...

We went to the Jackson Pollock art show the other day, by the way. At the MOMA — a museum you would love! Aunt Beatrice agreed to that one. (She got more relaxed about being out and about in NY as the days went on.) It was a J.P. retrospective which, as Bypass explained to me, is where they show every painting by the artist they can get their hands on, so it's their whole life on the walls, so to speak. I loved the paintings for their frantic energy and yet some of them really disturbed me. They started kind of gently and then, when he started to fling the paint onto the canvas, it was so angry and tormented.

93

They'd even built a full-sized model in the museum to show where Pollock worked. His studio was like a barn. The notes on the artist said it was real small, especially for someone who flung paint around like he did, in great angry sprays or those thick dribbles. But it was his own place, away from clean carpets and neat walls and even drop sheets.

All of a sudden I knew that's what I had to have. Not a barn, exactly, but a place of my own where I can work on my paintings away from the world. It was a revelation. I felt like I knew something I'd known all along, except now it was out in the open. An "outing," I guess you'd call it! I know I want to write — I always have, secretly and now not so secretly. But ever since I picked up a paintbrush — way back when the shrink said I should express my emotions, blah-de-blah — I knew I wanted to express something. Paint, it works out, is the most immediate way I know — the best!

And do you know what else? The most amazing painting in the whole show was one right at the end, in pride of place. It's called "Blue Poles" and it was fantastic to read that it was bought by an Australian art gallery years ago. Hey, how cool is that! So when it goes back there to Australia, you can go see it, if you haven't already. I'd really like to know your opinion of it.

Must get this away as we are actually into packing-up mode. I met this cute little dog in the park where I've been skating every day, and I've just got to get back this afternoon to say goodbye to him for the next few months. Oh yeah, to the dog's owner as well, who's a bit of a cute guy, I must admit.

(And no, Venny, I'm not a virgin. I thought you got that message about Carlo in Cannes. Not that he was the first or anything. The first was an absolute ... but that's another story!)

I feel kind of happier than I have for a long time, as if Aunt Beatrice is really being an aunt, including me, really like family, for the first time. Now all I need is a friend. Like you have Joel. And maybe Ros? Hey, and what about that Gayle girl? I feel there's something funny about her, but then how would I know?

With love

Sapphron
(Just tried it again — nah, I'll stay with Saffron)

PS. You're not thinking of a tatt, are you? I considered getting a frog tattooed somewhere secret. What d'you think?

PPS. I'm glad you still want to receive letters from me. And of course I'll keep on writing! The one from Bali should arrive super-fast.

Letter 14

6 January

Dear Saffron

Great to hear from you. Man, what a joke. Me go "up to Bali?" Sure, I live in Australia — a part of which lies in the tropics — but this place is the largest island continent in the world! Bali is like 6000 clicks from here. I thought you knew all about that sort of stuff. I should be calling you Sappy, not Saffy!

Anyway, it's good that old Aunty Beetroot has started to open up and tell you what's on her mind. It's a bit like "Days of Our Lives," I reckon. Missing sons and stuff. You'd better watch out. You might turn out to be your own sister. Or mother. That's what happens in the soaps. My mum watches them all. "Like sands through the hourglass ... "

Sorry. I hope that you get somewhere with the mystery. Honest I do. And if you do, I'll be here listening. Promise.

It's also good that you are doing some painting. No, I've never heard of Georgia O'Keefe, but my art teacher showed me a Jackson Pollock in an art book. Not really what I'd want hanging on the wall of my lounge room (I can just see it in Springvale — not!) but I respect where he's coming from as an artist, so good on him.

I reckon it's good if we can express ourselves creatively in some way. It might be rings through our ears or navel. It might be the cakes you bake. It might be our work. I mean, my dad's a panel beater but to him patching up beaten-up bumper bars is an art. Mum expresses herself best in her garden. Personally, I hate what she does. She's really into concrete statues — gnomes and stuff.

She said that now I've got muscles I should stand in the garden like Michelangelo's "David" statue in Florence, but maybe I'd end up looking like that Jackson Pollock painting — a big mess!

Anyway, you know what you wrote about the shapes in art pleasing you, like the old beggar was a person but also "shapes and lines?" Well, that's how I think of my body now I'm modelling. My body is like a work of art — line and texture, like you say — and mass and rhythm, but constructed from flesh and bone and muscle. I am learning to move these with a certain style. That sounds like pretentious rubbish, I know, and I'm trying not to be a poser, but it's how I see what I do. How I interpret modelling. It's an aesthetic thing. An art thing, just like I was trying to make in sculpture.

Some great news, I'm going for my driver's licence at last!

Ros Daniels, the PR agent for Svelte jeans and the main client I model for, has been giving me driving lessons in her BMW. The first time she came to pick me up at school was 4 o'clock one Friday afternoon. Trouble is, our school has an assembly every Friday arvo at 3:30. When assembly was over the whole school comes rabbling out and there's Ros in a black leather mini skirt, leaning on the bonnet of the Roadster. She's parked in the first bay of the administration car park, hasn't she? The principal's car park. What a blast! When everyone saw me go over and slide into the driver's seat and Ros slipped in beside me, my reputation went up a million points.

Ros says that I can use the BMW to take my test in a month or so. She says it makes sense to use the car you've taken your lessons in. I can't argue with that. Like, why would I want to?

Ros is very good to me. She introduces me to people and takes me places. She never talks down to me. She's 29 years old, I found out from Gayle. You said you thought Gayle was a bit suss. I think that was girl talk for "I should watch out for her." Right? Maybe she is a bit jealous of my relationship with Ros? Jeez, did I just say that? Babes jealous of being with little old Venny? Man!

But if it wasn't for Gayle going to the Formal with me I wouldn't have been spotted. "Discovered," as the pros say. Gayle could have any one of the male models if she wanted (except for the gays) so maybe she isn't jealous of Ros and me, just jealous of Ros' success and her clothes and her car, etc, etc.

But I just can't think about all that crap. All I know is that Ros is educating me — and man, was I dumb! She gives me grooming hints like what to wear to a particular venue or function. Classy! She corrects me when my language is coarse or inappropriate. She's also working on my accent. Especially my long vowels. She says Australians have very long, broad vowels and a rather embarrassing, unsophisticated accent that stands out like dog's balls in the modelling world. (I said that last bit, not Ros, hey!) Anyway, I really appreciate the changes she's making in me.

She never makes me feel like a kid, even though she is 12 years older than me and has had a heavy relationship with Brad Jones, the jock footballer (much more on him later — wot, me jealous?). She always offers me her arm when we're in public. She buys me dinner and classy little presents like underwear (OK, OK, Calvin Klein) and stuff. The other day when she picked me up she gave me a bottle of Chanel "L'égoiste Après-ravage." It's the dearest men's cologne and specially imported (like for male models). I know because I've seen it advertised in all the exclusive men's fashion magazines, like "Homme." I get Ros to meet me at a little café — make that the only café — in Springvale. I'd rather she didn't see mum's garden gnomes and the half-stripped car bodies that dad always has rusting away in the long grass in the front yard.

Anyway, after Joel saw me with Ros he came over home one day and we just hung out on the front veranda for a while like we used to. He likes to have a beer and a smoke and a yarn about old times. This was a bit different though. I mean, I can't talk to Joel like I talk to you about art and travel and stuff. He'd wet himself laughing. But it was pretty clear he knew that our lives were changing and we were growing apart. I guess he wanted to make contact before it was too late. He's a good mate, Joel. I've always liked him. All he wants is a laugh and a good time. So after an hour or so shooting the breeze (we were a bit smashed) he asked me if I wanted to go down the Football Club for dinner and a drink.

The football club is pretty rough and ready. Mostly working class guys and tradesman go there to get hammered. They talk about hotting up their cars and sport and that sort of crap. The management has a thing called the Happy Hour that goes from 6 pm to like 8 pm with cheap beer by the pot (big glass). A lot of pensioners go there too. They like the company, I guess, and the pokies and the cheap booze and the cheap food. When I said "dinner" before, I should have said that means steak and chips or meat pie and chips down at the Club. That's what "real men" are supposed to eat (I mustn't be a "real man," hey?). The meat pie is an Australian culinary icon. So you can probably work out that the Football Club is not really my scene. But this night when Joel asked me to go with him, I couldn't refuse.

I changed into a pair of good jeans and smartened myself up a bit while Joel talked to my mum and dad (like he does) and then we went.

Man, it was bad from the minute we walked in. The main socializing area is just one long bar with metal café tables scattered around and a wall of pokies behind them. Everyone was at the bar. The food wasn't "on" yet. The place was thick with cigarette smoke. I used to smoke but I don't any more. Well, maybe one Soubrani after a meal. But this was disgusting and there was that awful heavy smell of stale beer slops. All the guys were what we call Bogans. That means they were wearing cheap, badly cut, chain-store jeans, ugh boots (like knee-length sheepskin moccasins). They all wear heavy metal T-shirts tucked into their jeans and then a great big faded checked flannelette shirt (called a flanno) over the top. You can always see their packets of fags rolled into the upper sleeve of their flannos. Hair is long and greasy, or sometimes skinhead, with the odd tooth missing.

I have to admit that Joel wears this look like a uniform. It's not a good look, but it's Joel's label, if you know what I mean.

Anyway, Joel elbowed a place at the bar for both of us to squeeze into and ordered a pot. We drank and talked for a while and then I noticed this guy a few drinkers down catch my eye. A big guy, he was. Like huge. He was a cut above the rest, true. He was wearing a polo shirt and, from what I could see when he leaned back from the bar, a decent pair of linen walk shorts. There wasn't any doubt that he was checking me out and I started to feel really uncomfortable. Like threatened. I see a lot of gays in the modelling scene but they never try to hit on you. It's different here, though. I don't mean hit on you like for sex. I mean really hit you, as in bash and kick and punch. There's a really nasty butch homophobic undercurrent in the football club scene. And I was wearing designer jeans and a Fabiani shirt and I'd just had this George Michael style haircut, so I suppose I stood out like a sore thumb and was a sitting duck.

I gave Joel a nudge and asked him what was up this guy's bum. Joel took a look and said let's shift, OK? But just as we started to move this big dude gets up and comes straight for us. He comes and stands between me and Joel and right in my face. We were the same height but definitely not the same build!

He says, "You a model?" I sort of nodded and tried to push by but he blocks me again and says "Your name Vinny?" I said that my name was Venero and asked who wanted to know.

He said his name was Brad Jones and then I guessed what was going down. "I seen your picture in the paper with Ros Daniels the other day. You keep away from her, you ponce. I see you hanging near her again I'll cut ya nuts off. You get me?"

I tried to move away again but Joel heard all this and wasn't having any of it. Even though he was a good 30 cm shorter and like 50 ks lighter, he grabbed this thug by his arm and spun him around to face him. "If anyone's going to lose their balls it's you, fella," Joel says. "If you got any to lose, that is. You hear me?"

Jones hadn't been expecting any resistance, I'd say, and his face fell. I never saw such a weak cowardly expression. You could tell that he'd watched me and picked me for a wimp (true), but when he was up against this little guy who is like super-tough when he's worked up, I reckon he crapped his pants. Anyway he just said, "Yeah, well, he's been told, hey?" and slunk off.

So, you see, Joel and I might be drifting apart but I'd say he still thinks of me and I don't want to lose him. It's a hard call. I mean, one day when I'm famous, I might have to hire him as my personal bodyguard. Joke.

And speaking of relationships, no, I did not know that you had sex with Carlo in Cannes. I guessed you must be a virgin. As for Carlo, what I said about tight pants sticks. I thought he was just a bit of Italian dressing on the side, sort of thing. I'm stunned. You are a woman and here's me still a little inexperienced boy!

And what about that businessman you "picked up" in the hotel and had drinks with? Holy hell. You are bad, bad, bad, I think. I mean, how do I know that he didn't follow you into the lift and you know ... ?

By the way, did you look up the true meaning of the word romantic, like I asked you?

Well, if you didn't, it means, "seeing the mystery and wonderment of life. Imaginary, visionary or idealistic." Maybe that's me. Maybe I'm saving myself for the girl I love ... But then, maybe I just haven't had the chance ... Or I'm just a gutless wonder, afraid of rejection ...

I envy you going to Bali but one day I will get there, I just know it.

Anyway, tell me all about it for now and, as usual, I'll be fascinated.

Tonnes of love

Venero

PS. I really want to meet you, you know.

PPS. And since you told me a secret, here's one for you. My middle name is "Nero!" Vener-O Ner-O Merl-O. Oh! Oooh! Oooohhh! Get it? Unbelievable, hey!

PPPS. No tatts — I hate them!
   V.

Letter 15

Hotel Tjampuan
Ubud, Bali

6 February

Hey, Venny

Hail, Nero! I guess you know about the fiddle and Rome burning?

Good to hear from you and so quickly, even though your letter got sent on from New York. Things are happening fast here too!

Hotel Tjampuan, where we're staying, is one of the oldest established resorts in Ubud, which is up in the mountains in Bali. Temples and banyan trees and rice paddies everywhere! No, I won't do the travel-writing piece, I promise you — except I've just got to say this. Bali is a jewel of a place with picture book landscapes and gentle smiling people. (Well, in the hotels anyway. Outside is not quite the mayhem of India, but you can be accosted by some pretty enthusiastic and quite rude hawkers.)

I noticed at once that Bali's full of people with twangy accents. Not Americans, no — Australians. With lo-o-ong vowels, as you say. One guy who sat next to me at the Monkey Dance last night (which was fantastic by the way) told me you really do say "Ozzies" for Australians. And that some people, even your politicians on television, actually say "Austraylians!" It made me laugh. It'd be like ours saying Amerwicans or something equally pathetic!

"Ozzies" sounds so funny, too. And he said that's not all. For bathers you say "cozzies" and for mosquitoes you say "mozzies." He's an Australian (natch) and knows just where you live because he's from Brisbane too, only guess what he calls it? "Brizzy!" What a hoot!

Yes, I'm doing some sight seeing with him but it's just a holiday friendship. I don't want another Carlo type relationship on my mind, I can tell you. With Slade, it's like being with my brother, if I had a brother that is. And, by the way, that man in the hotel was just a flirtation with feeling grown up. Don't get the idea I'm wandering round the place cracking onto any man who might cross my path! I look at men — well, boys really — of course, just like you look at girls, but that's about it. It just seemed a cool thing to hang out in a bar in a swish hotel pretending. And writing you is a little bit like my diary. I tend to tell you a lot more than I mean to. As for Carlo, his name has from this momento dropped from my vocab!

In this hotel we have our own "losman." That is to say Aunt Beatrice is in a fashionable "hut" of her own (luxury bathroom, mezzanine floor and groovy veranda), as are Kevin, not far distant, and me.

I know I'm always talking about artists, but I've just found out that another Australian artist features here. Donald Friend (lovely-sounding name) lived up here at Ubud for many years. A bit like the painter Gaugin (whose work I adore), who went to live in Tahiti and fell in love with the place and the people. Kevin told me Donald Friend was gay and had affairs with the boys here. He sounded real disapproving. Mr Friend certainly did some wonderful paintings of the boys. In every losman in the place, Kev tells me, they have a coffee-table book of his artwork. I was lost in mine straight away — his line drawings are just fabulous!

Speaking of Kevin (he looks such a geek in shorts, you've no idea), he kindly set up my easel again and made encouraging noises about my painting. He suggested I get a portfolio together to impress Bea and the art school when we finally get back home. Says that's the only way I'll convince Bea to let me go there. The thing is, I just want to go off exploring with Slade, and mostly I get my way.

The strange thing about Kevin is that I reckon he could be gay. He was so disapproving and funny about that Australian artist that I thought, Uhuh, he protests too much. Just a hunch, but often those feelings turn out to be right, don't they? Anyway, as if I care.

Last night we had an exciting visitor at the pavilion where we usually eat. This woman called Heather (no other name given) turned up to meet Aunt Bea. Apparently she's the reason we're in Bali and, I suspect, the reason we went to India. She's a producer — some movies and lots of plays on Broadway. Without Heather, Aunt Bea managed to get mixed up with the wrong people altogether in Bollywood — or that's what Heather seemed to be saying. I just listened and tried like mad to get the gist of their rambling conversation.

After the dead end in India, Heather was obviously the reason we'd gone back to New York. And maybe it was Heather who had alerted Beatrice to the dilly-dallying of the private detective. He's been taking Bea for a ride for years and years, it seems, over her lost son — if that's what he's really investigating. I'm not sure yet and couldn't ask directly, but that's how it sounds.

This is Heather's time off from a hectic career, so it was pretty nice of her to get drawn into Aunt Bea's life in this way. She seems real keen to help her.

"Laurence was exceptionally talented, but of course he didn't stay long enough to really establish himself in Hollywood." That was just one of the comments Heather made about this mysterious son. She went on and on then about documentaries he made in Nepal and Tibet. So he obviously wandered the world. Like mother, like son, maybe?

When Heather started to say something about someone called Lily, I got the message I should retire so they could really talk, so I tactfully took my leave.

You won't believe this, but as I crossed the garden I saw Kevin and a young Balinese man walking towards — well, it could have been towards — Kev's room. Nothing more to report than that, but I just wondered. Though perhaps the young guy was a local painter (there are lots of talented artists here). Given how Kevin is obsessed by art, this could be the simple explanation, but you know ...

107

You certainly sound taken up with your modelling career, and that's great. It seems to me you're thinking of yourself more like a dancer, when you talk about the sculpture part of the work, than a model. I know you don't mean to be painful and I didn't take it that way, but I wouldn't let this kind of thing get around. The "Bogans" would make a meal of you, not to mention your competition. I'm glad Joel stuck by you in that Club place too. (It sounded scary and the big footballer guy didn't seem like the kind of friend that Ros would have? I mean, I know you said Ros and he had had a relationship, but from what you've said of him, it just doesn't seem to jell. He sounds crude and rude in every way. You'd better be careful!)

Venny, it was so cool to hear you use the word "aesthetic' (and spell it right!). Let alone give me a definition of romantic. (I think you are one yourself underneath all the other &*#* — a romantic, that is — I know I am.) Ros sounds good value taking such an interest in you, and I guess the aesthetic word might have been one of hers? I don't want to sound nerdy going on about words like this, but you are obviously a fast learner. Ros can see this and even though she stands to gain, so do you. In fact you have already, like Pygmalion. (Look that one up.)

Getting your letters is a bit like reading the chapters of a book these days. Everything seems to be changing for both of us! As you say, "Days of Our Lives ... "

Quick report!

It's a week later. After several afternoons with Heather, Aunt Beatrice seems all fired up about *something — travel plans again, I expect. Just when Slade had talked her into all of us visiting a volcano town!*

With love, and I'm glad we're physically closer, if you know what I mean. Maybe Brizzy next stop?

Love

Saffron

PS. I wonder what you're really, really like?

PPS. I know exactly where Australia is! I thought there might be cheap-as-chips holiday fares from Australia to Bali, like there are from LA to Hawaii. That's all! And you could have stayed with us. It was just a wild, silly, romantic thought.

Letter 16

12 March

Dear Saffron

You seem to be a lot happier than last time, but still in the dark about Beetroot's Quest, I understand. Who knows, you might turn out to be the only daughter of the missing Princess Anastasia, last of the Russian Romanov Dynasty! (Ros took me to a Classic Black-and-White Movie Festival a while ago and I saw Ingrid Bergman — all woman — in a movie called "Anastasia" about the missing princess. So that's how come I know.) Anyway it was good to hear your chirpy voice, so to speak.

And speaking of voices, you were pretty tough on the Aussie language, I reckon. I mean, you Yanks haven't got much to write home about, judging by the Americans I've heard speak. Talk about loud and brassy! You know, top models (the so-called supermodels) still seem to come from Europe, as does most of the haute-couture element of the fashion industry. Although there's a lot of US dollars poured into fashion, it's never really high fashion. The Yanks are better at accessible consumer labels like Levis. They sell billions, and make megabucks, I know, but they're not really class fashion! It's the same with their perfumes. Take the case of the US men's after-shave brand, "Tommy." I mean, it's not half as classy — or as sophisticated in its marketing — as Chanel's

L'égoiste or even Karl Lagerfeld. So, while the Ozzies might say "cozzie" and "mozzie" and sure, I might live in a town called "Brizzy," there's not a whole lot of class coming out of the States culture-wise either. I mean, you couldn't call Hollywood a High Culture export, could you?

Anyway, now that is off my chest, I admit that my own vowels are awful long and Ros has been working on that. You know, my "Aussie drawl." It's a dead give-away. Man, you should hear how "brooooad" Joel's speech is. He's what we call a "Dinkum Aussie." Ros says that if I am going to get International work (see much more on this later), I have to lose the accent. I saw a show on Elle McPherson the other night and I was really gob-smacked. She gave up Law at Uni to become a model and she speaks French fluently. I was impressed. Like really impressed. She is such a babe, too!!

It's funny, you know, that you mentioned "Pygmalion" in your letter. We are studying that play by George Bernard Shaw in English at school. Once upon a time I would have said it was all rubbish, but now I sit up and take notice. The story is from an ancient Greek myth where this guy fell in love with a statue and brought it to life. Shaw uses that in the play. We also saw the movie "My Fair Lady," starring Rex Harrison as Professor Henry Higgins and Audrey Hepburn as Eliza Doolittle. I thought the play was all right but I liked the movie better. Much easier to understand. The Pygmalion theme comes in when this street flower-seller girl (the statue in the myth) is changed into a cultured member of society by Professor

Higgins (Rex Harrison). The flowergirl becomes a lady who can "speak proper," if you like. I have to say that I liked her better when she was a flower girl. I thought she sold herself out to Professor Higgins, who was an uppity snob and an old fart. The word "prostitute" means to sell yourself for money, so I reckon the girl in "My Fair Lady" ends up a bigger prostitute than when Higgins thought she was one and she was just a simple flower-seller on the street. At least she had her integrity then. Although the original "Pygmalion" play doesn't end up the same way as the movie. Maybe that's because it was a Hollywood Yankee movie.

Just teasing.

But it's true that you can't get a good job if you're ignorant and uncultured and have no general knowledge of the world and can't speak properly or conduct yourself in public.

Those are the things that I owe Ros for. And you too, you know. You see, Saffy, you're my teacher too. Honest. You are. You might think all this correspondence is just a silly lovey-dovey teenage thing that we're playing, but you need to know that it's not like that for me. Apart from the fact that I really care about you (and worry about you sometimes — like with that Carlo louse and that Sugar-Daddy businessman you did pick up in the lobby of the Hanky-Panky Hotel wherever — don't deny it), and I think that you are good-looking, judging by your pictures (sexy too). Well, apart from all that, you've taken me around the world with you, and when you write about art and language you are teaching me. You're teaching me the way different people in different cultures behave and that breaks down barriers. It prevents xenophobia (look that one up!), and breaking down barriers is always healthy because it opens people's hearts and minds and so stops prejudice.

So, you are my Professor Henry Higgins. And so is Ros.

Anyway mega news.

No, I couldn't see you in Bali, even if it is "cheap as chips" to get there because I am saving my dollars for something — well, some things — else. Namely:

1. Ros has done a deal with an Italian Modelling Agency (Sfumato) and next year I am off to hit the catwalk in Rome and Milan and then on to Paris and London. Oh Yes!! Honest. Ros will take me herself as a sort of chaperone and while travel and accommodation are paid for, I'm still going to need $$$s to spend.

So I might be having cocktails with you in the Ritz or the Astoria or tea on Brighton Pier or somewhere. Who knows?

This is it, Saffy. This is the big one. No more Brizzy. No more Springvale. No more homophobic football stars. I'm off in six months. That's all. And believe me, will I make Eliza Doolittle look like a rank beginner! I am going to fly, Saffy. You just wait and see. Just watch your "HQ." Your "Ralph." Your "Vogue for Men." Yep, that will be me on the cover.

Maybe I'll even do the odd centrefold for "Playgirl," the way I'm feeling! (Just joking. Too tacky for me these days.)

2. I'm feeling this way for another good reason. I got my driver's licence last week. Ros came around after school and picked me up and we went to the test centre. I took the test in her BMW, like she promised. I think the Testing Officer was so impressed with her and the car that I needn't have turned on the ignition. But I did and I got it first time. I was high as a kite.

I've been squirrelling away some money for a car and there's a nice old red Alfa Sud Coupé in a yard down the coast. I can just afford it. I know I said that I'm saving to go abroad but I have to have my own wheels and I will have no trouble selling this neat little unit for the right price before I go. Like everything else from the continent, European cars are classy and maintain their value for resale.

But that's not the real news either.

The real news is that right after I got my licence, Ros said, "I think we should celebrate your success, so I'm asking you back to my place for dinner." I said sure. I mean it's not like I haven't been to her penthouse before, but this time she seemed to be a bit more anxious. So by 6 pm we were well and truly on the way to a good night. Feeling a little mellow after a few Scotches on her balcony, I was. After drinks she excused herself to put on the dinner and I just stared out over the city, watching night fall. So cool.

Then Ros called me in. Man. Wow. She was wearing this little black number (very short, very low cut) and the dining table was set with candles and flowers. Next thing she called "Garçon!" and a waiter all done up in black and white appeared out of nowhere and served the meal. Five courses. Five!! When we were finished Ros called him again and "the help" vanished as quickly as he had appeared.

When we were alone we took our coffee to the conversation pit in the lounge and settled down. Well, that's not true. Ros had been in a funny mood all night and she sat very close. Like on top of me. I thought "Uh, oh," and I was right.

I know that you are a lot more experienced in this sort of thing than I am, Saffy, so I needn't go into detail (not like Joel does!). Some people would say that we had sex (eg. Joel) but I don't think of it that way. I would prefer to say we "made love." For hours. Joel always said that it was all over in a couple of minutes and I guessed that would happen to me too, especially the first time. I mean, Joel told me that a lot of guys don't even make contact their first time and it's all over. Well, that didn't happen to me — to us — I'm happy to say. Still, it wasn't like we were in the back of a '78 Datsun Sunny parked outside my parents' house, was it? Ros has so much class. She knew what she was doing. She certainly took her time, that's for sure, and she taught me to do the same.

I took precautions, by the way. I've been carrying this pack of 'doms around in my wallet since I started modelling. How dumb can you get? I thought it would be Gayle Warning!!

So I'm not a virgin any more either, Saffy. How about that?

I haven't told anyone except you yet. I was going to

tell Joel but I changed my mind. Sure, like you say, Joel is a good friend and he bailed me out of my trouble with that football jerk (I don't understand what Ros saw in him either. I'm too afraid to ask. One day ...), but I had made a sort of a promise to go out with him on the night I got my licence. But Ros's offer was so sudden and too good to refuse. OK, OK. So I let him down. I can hear you accusing me from over there, wherever you damn well are. What else would any red-blooded Aussie male do? Hey? I suppose I'm wasting my time expecting understanding from a girl. I suppose now you think I'm the one "cracking onto" every female I see.

Sorry. OK? Sorry. I hate letting my mates down. I do. But — like I say, I had my reasons.

Anyway, when I rang Joel the next day to say sorry he was like chillin'. Bad.

So, just today I got onto him again and made him an offer I knew he wouldn't refuse. He couldn't refuse.

First of all, I asked him to pick me up and take me to the yard where they're holding the Alfa Sud. Joel just can't resist a used car sale yard.

And then I asked him to come up the coast with me in the Alfa next Saturday. Just the two of us. It'll be like old times. Just like we always said we would. I'll tell him I lost my cherry then. Hell, will he go ballistic. Like totally.

Only trouble is as soon as mum heard I had my licence and I was buying a car and I was going up the coast with Joel, she put on one of her prophetic turns. "Don't say you haven't been warned," she goes. "Don't say that you're not tempting fate. Blah, Blah and BLAH!!" Saffy, you don't know how lucky you are not having any parents!? Honest.

Your man in Australia (Today, that is. Tomorrow, the world)

Venero

PS. Let me know if (when) Slade cracks on to you (as I'm sure he will) and I'll drop everything and come over on a cheap-as-chips fare and punch his lights out.

The Big V. who is so-o-o-o excited!!

Letter 17

May 4

Dear Venny

Maybe, just maybe, I can talk Aunt Bea into Italy as vital for my art education and we could meet! "Seen at the Trevi Fountain: International Model, Venero Nero in Sfumato Jeans!" I'll wear look-alikes just to get into the picture. (Joke!)

But really, you cool dude, I'm so excited for you about Italy. Venny, this is a dream come true for you — an Australian dream maybe? Or maybe every kid everywhere wants to be good at something, a super something. Well, you are, obviously. You have fallen on your feet, in Gucci shoes and all! This is what we'd call the Big Break. And I can't think of anyone more deserving than you! Truly. Well done. Congrats, etc. Dreams can come true. Maybe more likely in Australia, come to think of it.

Not to bag my own country or anything, but it gets me down sometimes. You know the American dream that the Big Break is just around the corner. If you just keep trying real hard, that is. What a joke! It gives people such false hopes, I think. And it's an excuse for the filthy rich not to feel any responsibility for the poor.

118

Not that I can speak with a fairy godmother like I have now! But I do know the other side. Like just try a trailer park with a mother on welfare who drinks and eats too much, and see how many dreams come true. Let alone Harlem or skid row in any city or town. Hey, I want out of this downward spiral, I was congratulating you!

I think what's happened for you is fab. Your dreams of making the Big Time are sure as hell coming true, and Ros! Some chaperone for Italy. Mmm, they say lots of things about older women being excellent teachers in the art of love-making. You'll have to tell me all. It seems she's taken you on in every way. Despite your being a virgin, I think you're pretty insightful about lots of things — women as well. And anyway, I'm glad it was an OK experience first time for you. Half your luck! But just keep your wits about you with her. It's a bit like cradle-snatching, I think.

Wonder what the male equivalent of "Pygmalion" is? But I didn't mean you were an Eliza Doolittle. I've read the play by the great G.B.S. and the ending is sort of harsher than the film (although my Mom often said, "Beware you get what you want!"). The play is probably truer to life. You don't often get what you want. By the way, what you said about Eliza selling out was great. You can be DEEP, Mr Merlo!

Don't get your (Calvin Klein) knickers in a knot about the Ozzie accent and my comments, by the way. Read again! I didn't say I didn't like it. Not once! In fact I think it's kind of cute. But it's just a bit obvious.

And sure, American high fashion seems a contradiction in terms. But Venny, I've been pulled into so many of the European "name" shops I'm pretty well brainwashed with names and sick of brands, even if the clothes are to die for. It's the same ploy, whether it's Levi or Versace — buy it and see how happy, sexy, etc., etc. you'll be. Yeah, well, maybe for an hour or so. And maybe not! Bea gets mad when I dress in my Balinese batik wrap rather than my Gucci shorts. But too bad.

FYI (for your interest): Get this! I read somewhere that most people can't even identify 6 different birds in their locality or their country. But the average adult (you and me included) can recognize 1000 logos and labels. 1000! This article I read described us as "the culture of desire" and that was not meaning sex so much as wanting things. Everyone knows sex does sell things too, of course. The reason there are people like Ros out there looking for people like Venny out there! So I guess it's the same in Australia, hey?

Right now I don't care about any of it. I've just put my pen down for five minutes to look at the sunset — one minute thrilling terraces of rice and fringes of wild-looking jungle and the next the sun skids out of sight and an ebony night surrounds you. One that talks to you and looks at you too, no kidding. The night has a thousand eyes in Bali for sure. Slade tells me they are into the spirit world big time here — and there are plenty of bad ones ranging about, what's more. I'm sure he's right, 'cos they're buzzing around me now.

Nothing to report on the Beatrice side of things. Heather's gone. Lots of phone calls. And it seems we're going to Papua New Guinea (which is not far distant from Brisbane??) any tick of the clock. Sunday next in fact. And guess what — Slade says that PNG was on his itinerary and he might even join us there, although it's not so good for back packing because of the "rascals" there. (They have gangs just like we do in NY who go round robbing and doing the odd murder, but you probably know that. Aunt Bea says they're aren't any rascals where we're going to stay.)

Slade tells me there are some groovy and safe diving locations which are quite cheap. He loves skin-diving and has taught me about the wonders of the deep here. I've been diving three times now, and I just can't believe the extraordinary world down there! And that it's always there just under your feet and always has been! I'll never look at water the same way. I must say I want to paint some of the marvellous textures and shapes some time — they keep playing through my mind after we've dived. Not now though.

To be honest, I'm in a bit of a low mood tonight and your letter was the best thing that happened all day, although it's set me off on another painful train of thought. Kevin has been saying some pretty funny things to me again. He keeps dropping these little comments like, "You should work hard at keeping Beatrice happy. You stand to benefit, you know, as her grand-niece, that is if you play your cards right.'

I just said, as coldly as I could, "I don't know what you're talking about." To which he replied, "Well, you soon will." It made me feel cold all over, even here in the tropics.

I don't know why he's started on this tack again. but it's getting me down. It's almost as if Aunt Bea is going to throw me out or something. I know that's crazy. We've had three difficult years together but we've come through OK. I love that crazy, secretive woman most of the time, and I reckon she loves me now too. But Kevin's set me wondering.

And worse still, it only makes me think of Mom more and more, and I get that ice-pick-in-the-heart kind of feeling again. I miss her so much. It's hard to do anything but think of the good times with her. I torture myself going over and over the good times, until I nearly go mad! I want to scream and kick and beat my fists like the little kid I saw by the pool today. Boy was she having a tantrum! She was lying on the tiles and socking it to her parents. I was even jealous that she had two of them doing their darndest to console her when she probably needed a good dunking. Maybe I do too. I quarrelled with poor old Slade this morning and he went off by himself all day and I've been lonely and in a foul mood.

I couldn't settle. I couldn't even paint, and I attacked the notepaper a minute ago with a furious ugly scribble. And then I saw your letter and I even felt mad about that. But instead of scrunching it up like I meant to, I reread it and here I am. Writing. Trying.

Sometimes the Balinese night is so deep and I feel so far away from — well — from who? There's nobody for me but Aunt Bea, who's kicking back cocktails with some old biddies she's palled up with. But I'm filled with longing for something, for someone.

Sorry, Venny, to be so melancholy when you are so effervescent about life. I love that word "melancholy," though I don't like feeling it. Everything — even the

122

gamelan band I can hear playing in the distance and the giantesque crickets chirping away — everything is filling me with sadness. And it's so deep tonight I can't even cry, let alone scream like that little kid. I know I need to be close to someone right now and it's not Aunt Bea or Slade or Kev.

You are about to take flight and I wish you well. I really do.

With love and that indefinable something

Saffron

PS. You said such nice things about my taking you with you on my journeys. Just wish you were here right now.

PPS. Slade has just come and gone and cheered me up a little. Well a lot. Wait till you hear this. He says we stop down in Brisbane en route to PNG! Venny, here's a chance! I'll give you the flight times which I've just pinched from Aunt Bea's room:

Sunday, May 18, 4.30 pm. Qantas Flight 432. Fifteen minutes in transit and I'll be there. I'll recognize you, I know it! Hey, isn't this cool! I feel better already.

Be seeing ya!

Letter 18

20 May

Dear Venny

Where in the hell were you? I suppose you and Ros were off to some chic modelling gig and you forgot I ever existed! I was so disappointed you were not at the airport. It was hell getting out of the transit lounge and I could have been deported if they'd found out (or so Kevin said when he caught me sneaking back in). But I was sure you'd be there somewhere. I thought every dark-haired guy in blue jeans was you. Well, every good-looking one, that is.

Come to think of it, you and Joel are probably off somewhere "up the coast," as you put it. So I guess this letter won't be forwarded to you. But you've got to come home some time. So I'll still tell you what's happening here, as you can see by our address where we are.

We flew right over Australia from Bali, of course — and I must say when we first caught sight of land I felt real funny — emotional is another way of putting it. To know this was your country! It reminded me of the States in some parts — lots and lots of dry miles — but your desert was very different. And that bit all laced with water courses — so strange and empty — just streaked with these glinting water channels. It looked cool. And I kept thinking of you!

And then Sydney, all green and gorgeous, twining around those waterways. I wanted to stop there! I saw the Opera House — they said it is built like sails and it is. So graceful, perched right on the water like that. And the Harbour Bridge.

Then we went on to Brisbane, and while Aunt Bea was buying — you guessed it — duty free she doesn't need, I saw an opportunity. I managed to find an un-locked door and a flight of stairs and I just looked as official as I could and got into the regular terminal, which was like any other, I guess. But outside I could see palm trees and I wondered about Springvale and your folks and looked everywhere for you.

When ten minutes had gone by I realized you weren't going to show. I'd expected there'd be this cool guy there looking for me, and we'd recognize one anoth-er and ...

Anyway, it was dodgy as hell getting back into the transit lounge, I can tell you. Venny, where were you?

Write me now. Do you hear? We're moving on to Madang, so write c/o Madang Resort, Madang, Papua New Guinea.

Saffron

Letter 19

12 Acacia Drive
Springvale Qld 4035
Australia

30 June

Dear Miss Saffron Duval

I hope you don't think that I am rude writing to you like this but I am Venny's mother and thought that I should tell you what has happened to him. I am writing to you because your last two letters have been sitting on top of the china cabinet in our lounge room for weeks. One has been there even longer, maybe a month, and every time I walk past them I feel bad. Venny never got many letters except for yours. I always left them on top of the china cabinet and he picked them up when he came home, but yours are still sitting there and I know that he can't answer them so I thought I should let you know why not and what happened.

It is very hard for me to write this letter to you. In the first place I don't really know you except for what Venny has told me about you and that was all good, but I can't say I really know you, so that makes it hard. But the thing that makes writing to you hardest is that we might be losing Venny, and I can hardly think about it, let alone write about it.

Venny is in a coma after a car accident. He has been on life-support for nearly six weeks. It is his backbone. He has what the doctors call a T10 spine injury. In the old days they would say he broke his back. Nowadays the doctors use words that me and my husband Tony (that is Venny's father) can hardly understand and they talk to us like we were the dirt under their feet and not good enough to waste their time.

I have to ask you to excuse the smudges but I can't stop myself from crying. I am full of anger and full of guilt and also hurt, all at the same time. I will try and feel better and write better.

I have to say that I am sorry but I opened your two letters and read them. Now you know why Venny did not meet you at the Brisbane International Airport. But I did read how he must have told you how he and his friend Joel were going up the coast. Joel was killed in the same accident. Venny was the driver. You see why things are all upside down.

Now I have got that out I will start at the beginning.

Venny was making good money at his modelling. He had that offer to go to the old country with the woman he knew called Ros who was taking him. I have to tell you we did not like her. She wouldn't even come in our front door and she was too old for him. I don't know what was wrong with her. A woman as old as her with a boy is not right. But we were happy Venny was going over there. It was a chance for him. He was excited and he could look up some old places of our family. Many memories are there. But Venny wanted to buy this car before he went. He wanted to have fun, he said. Tony tried to stop him. Tony works with cars and wanted to help him pick one but Venny had his heart set on this one and that was it. It was his money.

127

The first weekend he got the car he was going up the coast with Joel. It was a promise and Venny said he owed Joel and when Venny makes a promise it is his word. It is in his heart and he will keep it. I was very worried about this weekend. I was always worried about Venny and cars. Joel was a nice boy and we all liked him and he was always welcome here in our home. He was good to us all, even to Tony's father if he was over from the Aged Home. Joel was wild but he was a good boy. He did crazy things and he liked the booze. He would drink too much and go crazy ever since he was 15 or 16 years old at High School but he was a good boy who would have made a good man. You will think that I am crazy too, but I know what I know and I had a bad feeling about this car, but there is no stopping young people nowadays and now it has come true.

They left our place Friday afternoon 6 weeks ago now and Venny kissed me and his father and his sister Teresa out in front of the house. I said to him, "Be careful, Venny," and that was the last thing I said to him. The police say that Venny was driving when it happened but not speeding or drunk. The road was wet after a storm and the tyres were baldy, as they say. If he had let his father pick out the car that would not have happened but Venny made up his mind he wanted this car that was going cheap. It was an Alfa. Venny only wanted things that came from Europe. He wouldn't look at anything that was made in Australia or the USA. He got all that in his head from modelling, but a lot of it came from that Ros he was seeing. She put ideas in his head. I will tell you now that we haven't heard anything from her since the accident was *written up in the paper and she hasn't been to the hospital once or phoned us here once. She hasn't even sent him a Get Well card, so we think that is the end of her. Teresa says that she might have phoned up the hospital and found out how bad he was and how he couldn't go to Italy so she dropped him like that and is finished with him. She is looking for a new boy, I think.*

The car skidded off the road and hit a tree on the highway. Joel had bad head injuries. They could not save him. He died in Emergency. We got a phone call from Emergency at 2 in the morning because it was 6 hours before anyone saw the car and got them out. We went straight down. It was very bad.

It wasn't just Venny, it was seeing Joel's mother who was there.

Venny was the driver, if you know what I mean. God forgive me for letting him go.

Joel has not got a father. He left years ago. It was very bad. I did not know what to say. It was my son who was driving. It was my son who killed her son and my son was alive.

Venny had his right leg broken, some broken ribs and his back. He was in a coma and still is. We don't know how long this will last but he could come out of it any time or it could last for months.

It is hard to get information out of the doctors. When we can find them and get them to talk they say the chances that he will be able to walk are not so good. That is because of where the break is in his back. The best thing the doctors say we can we hope for is that he can use his hands and arms. But what do doctors know? He is still full of tubes but his heart and his lungs are good they say. We do not know about other things like if he will be able to have children, if you know what I mean. That is all too soon.

I said this is a hard letter to write and we are still up in the air, as they say. I know from some of the things you wrote in your letter that you liked our Venny very much and I know that Venny always talked about you.

We can't say what will happen tomorrow and life takes twists and turns. That is how life is. It is no good saying I told you so. What is done is over and done. All the same, it is not all over yet or hopeless, and I light a candle for Venny every morning and every night and I ask you to do that as well wherever you are on the other side of the world. I know Our Lady will see it and know that we care and be kind to our boy.

I said that Venny was good with his promises and so am I, so I will make you a promise that the minute Venny opens his eyes I will write and tell you and then you can write to him again.

Thank you for reading this and remember our boy,

Maria Merlo
(Venero's mother)

Letter 20

10 July

Dear Miss Duval

I am keeping my promise. After 7 weeks and 3 days Venny is back with us. He is talking to us and using his arms and hands. His legs have no feeling. You can stick a pin in them. But still I thank Our Lady every day. So if you want to write to him you can and he can read it himself. I gave him your two letters to read and he laughed. It is good to see him laugh. His face is the same. He did not injure his face. He has the face of the Adonis, I always say, even if I am his mother, it is true and I will say it again. He has a beautiful face. You should believe me. But he does not know that Joel is gone. He keeps asking for him but the doctors say it is to soon to tell him. There is still more shock to come in his head and in his body so we must protect him.

I told him that I promised to tell you when he came out of his sleep and he said to say Hi and so I am. He said to say "You better damn well write." That is exactly what he said so I repeat it exactly.

You must have lit a candle too because our beautiful boy is back with us. Thank you from our hearts. If you write Venny a letter don't write about Joel. He will have to find out one way or another but in a letter is not the way.

If you light a candle now, light it for his legs that he can walk again. If this is possible for our boy we still do not know.

Thank you.

Maria Merlo

Letter 21

Madang Resort
Madang
Papua New Guinea

July 17

Dear Maria Merlo

Thank you so very much for thinking to write to me during this terrible, terrible time you are having! I thought I would faint with fright as I was reading your news about that car crash and about Venny and his friend Joel. I cannot imagine how you and your husband and your daughter Teresa felt when you got the news — and how you still must be feeling today. My blood ran cold, and I was already praying for him before I'd even finished the letter. And then I cried. But when I got your second letter and heard that Venny is with us again and that he has even read my letters and laughed, I gave such a whoop of excitement my aunt came running.

Mrs Merlo, I have taken the liberty of writing to Venny and enclosing the letter in your envelope, because you said he wants me to. I haven't ever met your son, only by letters as you know, but already I know that he is very dear to me. Someone to be cherished. And of course I will continue to say prayers and hope that his fighting spirit will help him through whatever happens. Sometimes, when your dreams are smashed *the way they have been for Venny, it can bring out the best in you. I know that probably sounds trite to you right now and I wouldn't dare say it to him — well not directly — but I believe it.*

You are a very kind person to tell me exactly what happened the way you did, and even of the death of Joel, which is a shocking thing for everyone concerned, but very much for Venny, who may feel responsible? I suppose that's why you are asking me not to mention it. I have been through a death and it's the hardest, the most bitter thing to experience that there can possibly be. I know that he'll need a lot of care, and if there is any way I can help, please let me know.

I will talk to my aunt about allowing me to come to Brisbane, but though I'm not hopeful of that happening just now, with her life in a bit of turmoil too, please know I will do my utmost. More than anything I just want to be with your son.

I have found a church not far from here. I've got to tell you I'm not religious, not after my Mom dying the way she did. But because of your letters, I'm going there every day and lighting candles for Venny. I do have a strong feeling that he is going to come though all of this and I'm not sure why. But I feel so helpless far away from him and all of you who are going through so much. I know that you are very brave from your letter and you've helped me to be brave too. I must admit that I am frightened, but at the same time, I am filled with hope for Venny.

Yours sincerely

Saffron Duval

134

PS. Mrs Merlo, I don't know why I should say anything to you at all, given what's happening in your life and in your son's life right now. But I have the strongest feeling it will be OK with Venny, as I said before. I won't tell Venny just yet, but things here in Madang with my aunt are not good at all. It will probably mean that we head back to the States sooner than we thought. I've been telling Venny about this merry-go-round-the-world we've been doing in search of something. She's found the something —well, it's a someone — and since then everything's changed. That's all I'll say and please don't think you have to write back or anything — your hands will be full, I know. But if I don't come to Brisbane it's not because I'm running out on Venny and I wanted you to know that.

PPS. I wanted to call Venny on the phone immediately but my aunt spoke to a doctor who's staying here and he has suggested I leave it for a week or so? I don't want to wear him out with talking, as I realize it's probably an effort, like everything else.

Letter 22

Madang Resort
Madang
Papua New Guinea

July 17

Dear Venny

What a mess you've found yourself in right now. But how wonderful that you've come a long way through such a terrible experience. What a miracle in fact! I couldn't bear to think of a world without you in it! And now I don't have to — you've come back! To your family and to me. And here I was thinking you were raging with Ros and I was forgotten! I feel so guilty about my last letter — please tear it up. Oh Venny, I just want to be there, sitting beside you, helping you come through the pain and the shock of all this, if only I could!

Your Mom has told you she wrote me and I cried buckets when I got that letter. I was beside myself with shock at her news. All the poor-little-me thoughts I'd had fled out the window and into the deep blue (which is all around because we're in a resort in Madang).

Thank God for her second letter that told me you were conscious again and already able to talk and even move! My thoughts and my love flew to you then. To Australia, to Brisbane, right to Springvale. And all my energy too. I've been lying in bed at night, willing and willing you to get better, Venero Nero Merlo — so you'd just better get on with it.

When you can write — and I know that will be soon — please tell me anything you want to about what's happening. I want to know and I don't mind being a sounding board because in a weird way I have this feeling I can help you through this.

Madang, you ask — what's it like? Well, we arrived on a small plane at a very small airport. One tin shed, very hot, and the Hertz car hire place was an even smaller tin shed outside. But I smelled the heat and the tropicality (if there's such a word) in the air and I was in love with the place at once. We drove (in our small, hot, hire car) up roads with towering palm trees either side (must be the tallest in the world), and then thick bushes, which the guide told us were cocoa trees. (They make chocolate out of cocoa beans.)

As we came to the resort I glimpsed the sea, which was a magical blue. There's a huge, thatched, open dining-room area, very much like Bali I suppose, except that outside at night several "guards" walk up and down through the thick trees. You're not going to believe this, Venny, but they're armed with bows and arrows. Anti-rascal weapons! I mean I'm glad it's not guns as it would be at home, but bows and arrows! I asked to look at them and one of the guards was proud to show me the cruel metal tip. A dangerous weapon for sure, if you knew how to use it, and he obviously does. (Even here there are warnings about going out alone at night, which is very sad, because the outdoors is calling to you all the time, night and day.) But people still do. If I go out to stargaze I make a hell of a lot of noise in case the guards get the wrong idea and I find an arrow stuck in my back!

Everyone has a small bungalow with a tiny front veranda, much less glamorous than Bali but very comfortable. Mine is only a few steps from the water and I can slip into the sea and bathe on first waking (well, before the dreaded Algebra lessons). With diving gear I just glide and explore another amazing underwater world. I can't seem to get enough of this truly rapturous place and would stay all day (turn into a fish for real) if I was allowed. The coral and the plant life are more dense than in Bali and the colours once again quite extraordinary. A stingray floated by today — huge but undulating placidly and not interested in me in the least. I didn't turn a hair, just floated by too. A school of fish swept right over me. The most vivid blue tiny specks of fish you can imagine. I think they think I'm a rather largish one of them, for they simply swarmed all around me. For hours on end I am lost in this calming, spectacular world! Not quite lost though. Before I knew about you, I used to just let the underwater run through my mind at night like a video, and I've never had such cool, beautiful thoughts. But now you are on my mind all the time.

I had this great idea this morning! Maybe it would be good for you, when you are a lot stronger, to come up here or at least get to the seaside where you could swim? It would strengthen your arms and legs. I think of you constantly, you see, even when I'm swimming. Venny would like this. Venny would love that! I see you here, I really do! I know this might even sound cruel when you're still stuck on a bed, but somehow I think if you can believe the best, it's for the best.

There's some stuff going down with my aunt but I'm not going to bore you with that, Venny. In fact I don't want to go on and on. Even reading this might tire you out at present. I just want you to "see" the light and beauty of this place and imagine us scuba diving here together. We can do that, Venny, I'm sure we can one day.

Kevin (whom I've also told about your predicament) said it will be a hard time for all of you. He should know. He revealed for the first time ever something about his family. He told me that he has a younger brother who was in a car crash two years ago, and it was months of recuperation for him. He was quite emotional, which was a shock because Kevin doesn't usually show his feelings. He got a bit teary suddenly and it was strange, because it was right when he was telling me his brother is OK now. Yes, this same boy (Dean), who took months to come through all of the effects of his injuries and

139

who couldn't walk for weeks and weeks, is FIT AND WELL now. And studying engineering. So just think of that!

But if you're real down, which you might be because getting well again is sure to take time, just think of me thinking of you. I'm thinking of you right now and I'm sending you kisses. Lots of them.

With love

Saffron

Letter 23

Nowheresville

15 August

Dear Saffron

You write that you're sending me kisses but you wouldn't if you could see me. My life is over, I tell you. Rooted. Stuffed. I've got tubes coming out of every part of me, they shaved my hair off, I pee through a tube, I crap in a nappy, I'm lying here waiting for my useless legs to shrivel up (muscular atrophy, you call that. I'm learning a whole lot of new words now. Ha, ha). And I only found out two days ago that I killed my best friend. How's that for starters? You sure you still want to kiss me? I wouldn't even want to know me.

I'm a vegetable, that's what I am. No girl in the world is ever going to look sideways at me ever again. I worked that out pretty quick. And even if my hair does grow back like they say and I get to control my bum and my bladder, like who in their right mind would want to go with a murderer? And you might as well know they told me today that I might never crack a woody again, if you know what I mean. Like ever get it up again in the boys' underwear department.

Life is a boil, that's what it is. A boil full of pus.

Mum keeps saying, "Pray to God. Pray to God for help." Sometimes she says, "Pray to God for mercy."

Sometimes she says, "Pray to God and thank him for his blessings." She says, "You could be dead."

Yeah, right. Thanks for taking my legs away. Thanks for taking my life away. Without my legs I AM dead. You ever seen a catwalk model on crutches? You ever seen a catwalk model in a wheelchair? Believe me, if there is a God he must be laughing now, because he did a really good job on me. Set me up and offered me the world — note that I say OFFERED — he didn't quite get around to GIVING it to me. He just let me SMELL it, then he cut me down. Like literally.

I wish I was Joel, that's what I wish. I wish it was me who was killed and not him. So thanks for the best wishes and the kisses and the fruit basket and the grapes (ha, ha), but they're no good to me.

If you could send me Joel so I could hear him laugh and be stupid just one more time, and if you could send me my legs so I could get into a pair of jeans again, I'd say great, but since you can't, and no one can, I'm saying thanks for the memories. Writing to me is a waste of time so don't and so long. I hope you have a better life than mine. Just forget about me.

Venero

Letter 24

Ward 2 North
St Lukes Hospital
PO Box 420
Logan Qld 4230

22 August

Dear Saff

Sorry, all right?

Sorry, sorry, sorry. I didn't mean to hurt you. It's just that stuff is falling so thick and fast here that there are days I just want to kill myself and I would except that the hospital-issue steak knifes are too blunt. Joke. The latest thing is that the cops rolled up talking manslaughter charges. Like thanks, guys, and here's me just days out of a coma. Anyway, all the snooping and questions came to nothing since there was no evidence of speeding or grog. The Alfa tyres were a bit worn — but not bald — and the car had a roadworthy certificate when I bought it only days before so it wasn't dangerous driving or negligence. It was an accident. That's what I have to get through my head. It was an accident. Like I said, I would rather be dead than Joel. I would give anything to have him back. It's not like I did it on purpose or was being a hoon. It was an accident. OK? So the cops didn't push it. What would it prove anyway if they did get me for manslaughter? Being locked up for 5–7 couldn't be any worse than being legless. Could it? (Also a joke.) You have to learn to laugh at all sorts of sick things in here, like ha ruddy ha! when the brown stuff dribbles out of your nappy. Big joke.

OK. I'm not going down the death row trail again. I'll try real hard to be nice.

You want news?

Well, the situation is that I have a T10 spinal injury. That means that there is a lesion (break) at the 10th thoracic segment of my spine. My lower back.

This lesion or break is not "complete." That means there is hope that I will regain the use of my legs. (I don't count on it and the doctors say don't count on it too.) That means that I might be able to get an erection and ejaculate sperm and lead a normal sex life. That much they say I can get my hopes up about. Things look good in that department. There's been some stir-ring in the night, if you know what I mean. (Another time I'll tell you how they test if my willy is working. It's a bit rude!) I hope they're not just kidding me to keep my spirits up because if I find out they have I'll top myself. I will. They keep saying that they don't know everything yet because my body is still in shock and the nerves sort of "freeze up."

Anyway, as I am writing to you, you can tell that I must have the use of my hands and arms. I have what is called a "skull calliper" fitted to my head, which is why they shaved my head. The skull calliper is a band of steel that adjusts pressure on my skull and that transfers to my backbone and relieves pressure there or something. Some of the stuff the doctors say is over my head — like literally because I'm lying down (joke) — but I understand most of what they say. They also fool around, saying things like, "How's every little thing?" when I know they mean my dick, you know, but they're cool. They do try and tell me the truth, I think.

They didn't at first. Nor did mum and dad. I was really hacked off about that. I guess they were right not to tell me. Being in shock I didn't need to know the whole story. I mean, I wasn't ready to cope with all that at once, but there sure as hell better not be any more bad news they're holding back on.

Mum and dad are good but they still drive me crazy. They just can't relate to the doctors. They always think that the doctors think they're stupid and laugh about them behind their backs. I can't see that but mum and dad do get all the anatomical terms wrong all the time and mum really wants to rub my back and give me a sponge bath — YAAAA!

I guess things must be looking up because I saw a really good-looking nurse yesterday (looked a bit like you, actually), but she massaged the guy next to me instead, lucky sod. I guess I still look too gross, with this calliper on my skinhead and my pee-pee tube running into a bottle under the bed, for her to get too interested.

So how come I can write letters is that I'm allowed to be sat upright for two hours a day. I'm in one of those special beds they call a profiling bed that the nurses can adjust. Right now I am sitting upright. They asked me if I wanted to play computer games or something but I said if they had a computer could I write a letter. I wouldn't be too confident writing one by hand though. So they brought me in this keyboard and put it on my tray table but they have suspended the monitor in special adjustable brackets over the bed. It works OK.

I still drink out of a dribble-proof cup or use a plastic straw, but at last I have been taken off the mush food (I had a drip at first) and am allowed to have proper food that I can cut up myself. Pathetic, hey? But the food is OK. You actually get offered a menu.

I still go down bad some days. They are terrible. I think about what I had and I can't get over that it's gone forever. I can't get over how God tricked me. How he just gave me a taste of success and the good life, then said that's all you're getting, bang.

I saw this movie once at home with mum. It was black and white and had Rock Hudson in it. It was called "All That Heaven Allows" if I remember right. It was about this really daggy, plain Jane, spinster, old maid who falls in love with Rock Hudson and she never believes that a cool guy like him would fall in love with her (in real life he wouldn't have but not because she looked crook but because he was gay. Ha. Another joke). Anyway, in the movie he does fall in love with her and she is like totally headless because she never thought that he'd ever take any notice of her and she's saying, "Thank you, God, Thank you, God," and then he gets killed in an avalanche. See? Like the title says, that was "All That Heaven Allowed" and I reckon God saw all the good things coming my way and said to himself, "Sorry, mate, that's all you're allowed," and that was it. Bang. It was too good, see? And he doesn't want humans getting too happy. See? It's like life's a dirty trick. At least, that's what I reckon.

Anyway, there I go again so I better stop. I am really sorry that I dumped on you. What you wrote was beautiful. True. It meant a lot to me. No. It means a lot to me. I don't know if you know or not but Ros dumped me. Never seen or heard from her once and it's not like I didn't get mum to leave her messages, but no reply. And mad Joel's gone. I don't expect I'll see any of my modelling friends. I tell you, I knew way back that models were a self-centred lot. If their "friend" got a cold they wouldn't go near them in case they caught it. Models can't stand being near people unless they have health and perfect bodies like theirs. It's like too embarrassing to be seen near a fat person. So I don't expect to see Gayle Warning near a legless one.

So you're it, Saff. Well, that's not true. There's mum and dad and Teresa and you. And grandpa. He came up to see me with mum and dad, and even though he's loopy he told me that he saw guys cut up more than me in the war and they came through. I thought, yeah, right, Gramps. Like hell, but the thought was there. He's a sausage short of a barbie, but he's a good guy.

Please write to me. Tell me everything like you did before and try to pretend that nothing's changed with us and I still look like I used to in my jeans ads. Pretend. OK? I want to know about that old bat Aunty Beetroot and what she's up to and where you're going. You can be my legs and travel the world for me because I'm sure as hell never going to do it. You do that for me. Right?

Thinking of you

Venny

Letter 25

Madang Resort
Madang
Papua New Guinea

2 September

Venny, Venny, Venny

Before I tell you anything at all I just want to say one thing. You've got guts, you really have! And that's going to get you through — all of us through. I don't need to pretend about you because you are still the person you are, and that you were. In fact maybe even more so ... now that sounds confusing, doesn't it? You've been forced to grow up in the most terrible way (the way I had to).

Oh Venny! How my heart aches for you about Joel. Accident or not, I know how you must feel. The way my Mom did about Dad. My Dad came back to try to patch things up and she said (and was probably right) that he was just back to get more money out of her. Anyway, they had this slanging match and he flew out of the place and drove like a bat out of hell and smashed up the car and died and she never saw him again. At first she thought it was her fault entirely and it really made her suffer, but then she realized it was a whole set of circumstances, not just one. At least you know it was an accident and not your fault, and I'm so glad the police are going to leave you in peace to get over this thing. You'll miss him so much, like I miss my Mom, but try to think of the good things and the funny things between you and Joel when the black moods come down — and they will — as you already know, my dear and darlingest friend.

Your letters, of course, made me cry and then laugh and then bawl all over again. And then I thought how wonderful it is that you need me — I mean really need me. I'm glad someone does, Venny, because things sure as hell have gone sour here.

Hospital must be awful, what you're going through, and maybe the immediate future looks goddamn awful too, if not impossible! Lying there waiting and hoping must be so hard for an active person like you with the promise of so much. But don't give up hope — that lesion thing, though I don't know what it really means, doesn't sound hopeless. And even if (I won't say the words), even if things don't turn out as well as you want, look at the stories of some of the people who've had terrible accidents — say like Christopher Reeve. He inspires the world! And you're already way better off than he is — you can move and write and do all kinds of things. You can already take an active part in the world. All right, it's easy for me to say but I just thank fate, or God or whatever, that you're there, and thank you for your fighting spirit!

The truth of the matter is I need you right now, too. So here's what the end of the journey has brought for me. It's a long story but I'll try to make it as short as possible.

Aunt Bea, as you know already, has completed her search of the world and she's found what she wanted to find — or the person she wanted to find. Kevin was trying to warn me there might be this big upheaval in my life, but I guess I just couldn't believe it would go like this. Of course, Aunt Bea and I have had rough patches, but I thought that was only normal. Looking back, I know a lot of it was my anger and hurt that I was dumping on her. I was a difficult teenager, I know! But she's turning out to be the teenager in her emotions now.

Her son Laurence apparently shocked the pants off his parents way back when, taking on a partner who was not only black, but wasn't even American — or should I say African-American. In those days that was just undreamt of for someone like Laurence's family. She was a New Guinea girl who had never been out of her village. Laurence sailed into Port Moresby (a hot-shot sailor and at that time an over-indulged son) and fell head over heels with this girl. He met her through some trading company who were there mining gold and who'd decided to sell things to the locals on the side. (E.g. they cut up the pages of the Australian newspapers, since no one could read them, and sold bits to the "natives" to roll their cigarettes. As you can see, very enterprising! She worked for them doing this.)

Not only was Lily (that was the name Laurence gave her) "native," but she couldn't speak much English at first, and was probably under age (all this from Kevin of course).

The minute Laurence's father (Bea's revered husband, Tom) learned of his son's plans to marry Lily and

151

bring her home to the States, he told him to break up the liaison. I mean, Laurence's plan was a bit insane, because in those days there were separate schools, shops, buses and even toilets for white people and coloured people. Martin Luther King and plenty of others were trying to bring about some sort of equality — but you probably know he was shot dead for his trouble. It was a tense time in our history and there were race riots all over America.

So, to bring home an uneducated (Western-style, that is) and timid girl was crazy and also cruel (to her, I mean). Anyway, the parents went ballistic when Laurence told them his plan, then when they'd calmed down slightly, they tried another tack and called in the family lawyers to advise him, which made him go ballistic in turn. They threatened him with what was dearest to their hearts — their worldly wealth and his inheritance. (I see now money is Beatrice's measure of meaning and affection, and of course her power.)

Laurence went against his parents' wishes all the way and, to cut a long story short, his father disowned him. And, come to that, his mother! (I just can't imagine this. I mean I hardly had model parents. I know my Dad played around and wouldn't support Mom or me, but even at our worst moments there's no way my mother would have given up her only child.)

Then Laurence and Lily had a son, Harry, and Laurence decided pretty quickly not to go back home with them. Things were very bad in the States by this time. Laurence and Lily travelled around on his yacht, and the funny thing is, Venny, Laurence ran a little courier business between PNG and Australia for some years. It was all a bit of a struggle for him and Lily, but when he had some money again, he went back into film-making. But the story doesn't end happily — at least not for Lily and Harry.

Laurence apparently fell in love with a young New Zealand woman who had to come to PNG to do a documentary on dance up at Goroka. He became involved with the film, which went on for months, and then involved with her. She was of a wealthy landed family in New Zealand and Kevin said he imagined that Laurence must have slipped back into a familiar easy lifestyle with her. Anyway, he left Lily and his son and went to New Zealand with her. They had a daughter, Diane. (Are you still with me — it's kind of complex with so many names!)

Laurence still travelled far and wide on his yacht and made many powerful documentaries — got quite a reputation. He even worked in Hollywood for a while, but he never contacted his parents again.

Funnily enough, this New Zealand daughter, Diane, became a film-maker like him, and she was a sailor too. Eventually she learned that she had a half-brother — maybe her father told her in a fit of guilt. Whatever, she wanted to meet her New Guinean brother and she made a fatal trip to link up with him.

Apparently Aunt Bea learned all this on good authority from the movie fraternity she tapped into — mostly from the mysterious Heather who visited us in Bali. It turns out that Heather was a friend of Laurence's!

It's so damned dramatic, it reads like a fairy-tale — a gruesome one. Diane was killed in a terrible volcanic eruption here. She went in, camera-happy, when they told her the rumblings were not over and apparently it was the dense smoke and soot fall-out that killed her. Congested her lungs. She never met her half-brother.

Laurence died broken-hearted. He didn't ever really know his son Harry, who died in his twenties in PNG of a tropical disease complicated by malaria. God, talk about a Greek tragedy! Well an Antipodean one, anyway.

Now it seems that, in all her expensive detecting work (the more recent stuff anyway), Beatrice finally got wind of Harry. As she'd always suspected, there was something of Laurence to be found in the form of offspring, and suddenly she wanted kinship big-time. Then Bea found out that though Harry was dead, he was survived by a daughter. So Bea discovered she had a great-granddaughter in PNG, a direct line to her only son.

Why all this suddenly came up, I can't imagine, but maybe it was all about something Françoise told me. She said that Bea had a heart scare about ten years ago and after that became obsessed about her son and heir and his (read her) "line" not dying out alto-gether. That's why she took me in, even though I was only a distant rel. I was a distraction, it seems, but only that. I was nowhere near as close to her son as she would have liked.

The news must have broken when we arrived at Madang, I realize now, because last week we were given a special welcome dinner. The whole village turned out

154

and did a dance and then this girl called Lema was "presented." She turns out to be Harry's daughter!

Well, it was love at first sight with Beatrice. She said Lema looked very much like her son. (Apparently brown skin is no longer a barrier — my, how time changes everything.) And she is very pretty and vivacious, I must say.

This is the strange bit, Venny. Aunt Bea lost all interest in me the minute Lema came on the scene. She seems entranced by this girl, who I must admit is appealing and obviously quite smart. But now it's almost as if I don't exist.

The worst of it, Kevin tells me, is this. Bea's called in the wretched lawyers again and apparently she's completely rejigging her will. What do I care, I hear you ask? I don't really care and I didn't know until now that anything was left to me anyway. But it appears that Park Avenue, the Impressionist paintings, the shares, stocks, bonds, the whole caboodle, were all going to be mine! Well, now it seems it's all Lema's (that's what Kevin heard), and Lema is coming back with us to New York next week!

I'm not sure where this leaves me — back in a trailer park, I guess. So you can see why I feel all over the place, too. Aunt Bea is not interested in anyone else — just Lema. She's made that perfectly clear.

Compared to your problems, my darling Venny, I know this is nothing. You are going through stuff I can't even imagine and in all of this my heart goes out to you. It really does. But I feel this misery about Aunt Bea I can't explain exactly. Well, I can. In a word: betrayal! It's

155

not about the money for me. I've been poor and it looks like I'll be poor again. It's how she's turned off her feelings (love? even affection) that hurts so much. She's just gone cold on me. Now I come to think of it, she must have done that to her son, too. She can hardly bear to talk to me, she's so enthralled with Lema.

It's sickening really, but her eyes brighten the minute that girl appears. And Lema's such a warm person. She throws her arm round cold Aunt Bea's shoulders and kisses her, and Aunt Bea positively purrs! I can't bear to be around them, though the girl is sweetness itself to me! Yes, of course I'm jealous. I feel almost as bad as I did when Mom died.

So you see, I need your help and, dare I say, your lovely warm and honest opinion that I am so used to. You are the Venny I always knew — nothing has changed for me, for your letters still come full of humour and doubt and hope and zest for living. You are one and the same Venny to me, and I don't give a fig for your modelling career and neither should you. Your Mom is right in saying that a lot of those folk are totally insincere — and that's been borne out with that Ros, now hasn't it?

So we're both in a bad place right now, and OK, yours is a real bad place. I won't be coming by to see you, Venny. I wanted to but Aunt Bea won't listen to me and she seems in a real big hurry to get back to New York. I should go with her, because Kevin says I need to know what's going on with the rest of my life, and let's face it, I haven't got a cracker of my own to do anything else but go along with her. For the moment that is.

Maybe I wouldn't be much of a help to you anyway.

But my feelings for you are stronger by the hour, and I just know that we are going to meet one day. A day that's not too far off.

Let's just keep writing for the moment — I know it's helping to keep me sane.

Be brave as I know you are.

With love and lots of it

Saffron

PS. My suspicions about Kevin being gay were correct (I'm very sensitive to these things). He's not coming back with us to New York. He's told Aunt Bea that he's going to Bali to live with "a friend." But he told me the truth. He said he didn't know that he was gay until now — or not really — and he's fallen in love for the first time in his life. He's got a tutoring job in Bali just to be near the young man.

Even though he was pretty dry and boring to begin with, he's turned out to be a real friend to me, giving me good advice. He seems to care something about my future, and shows it in his awkward way. Isn't life strange?

Letter 26

14 September

Dear Saffy

Wow! I had a feeling that old Aunty Beetroot was up to no good. It's really none of my business, but what a cow! How could she just dump you like that after all this time? I know people say that blood is thicker than water (or something) but how could anyone just throw you off like you were someone she met for 5 minutes in a train — or a quickie behind the boys' toilet block, as Joel would say? It can only mean one thing — that she's a user with no heart. She was just letting you hang around like a back-up in case the real thing — the blood rellie —never showed up.

It means also that she's such an unfulfilled human being to need the (artificial) boost of a family blood line to make her feel important — no, to make her feel alive. And that's terrible. Believe me, we are who we are and we are all ultimately alone. You have to be really down to learn that. You have to be stripped of everything. You have to face yourself. I reckon that old Bea has never had to do that. She's still living in the delusional state of thinking that money can solve everything and buy everything — like a family in her case. Like happiness and personal fulfilment even. Boy, is she going to be proved wrong. I don't mean that as a threat or a curse, just as a fact of life.

OK, OK. I know that heaping it all on her isn't going to make things better for you. Abusing her from here (like I'm 3 continents away) isn't going to change a thing. No, she's made her decision, she's made her move and that's that — but what a move it was. What a power play! Still I won't go over it again. You must be sick in the guts over it all without me rubbing your face in it. Besides, she's not going to change now and anyway, if she did, even if she came crawling back, sucking up to you, you would have to be really stupid to listen to her. You would have to forfeit all your self-esteem to ever trust her again. But still I'm worried about you. You will have to face a lot of changes. To make a lot of changes. It's you who has to accept those changes and come through.

And don't I know all about that!

I think I've become the world's master at making changes. Boy, did I have attitude! Did I spew about "my lot" as Father De Lesseps called it when he came to visit. By "my lot" he meant like having what "the Lord deals out to you," as he called it in his nice soft voice. In my case "my lot" must mean: no dick and no balls and no legs and no friends (like I killed my best one) and no job and no life and no future, etc, etc. "That's how God tests us," he told me (he was holding my hand and looking into my eyes), "but He only tests those that He loves and they will find peace in Heaven."

So I said, "Well, Father, since you've got legs and a job and everything (I didn't say anything about a dick and balls because I don't think the Good Father has got, or ever did have, any genitals), so since you don't seem to be suffering (De Lesseps must weigh 140 ks), doesn't God love you?"

Then he says, "Ah, my son, judge not that ye be not judged," and that's when I told him to get lost. (Well, I actually didn't say that. I told him that I just filled my nappy. He sure took off then.)

What I mean about me making changes is that I don't really have any choice. I have to accept change. What the hell option have I got? No matter how I moan and whinge, I'm never going to make my legs work again. They're rooted. They're like two dried up sausages dangling off my pelvis. Still, in spite of what I said to the Father, I guess I should tell you right off that I just found out that there's not three dried-up sausages AND a couple of shrivelled-up olives dangling down there too. Yep! That's right, Saffy, I'm OK in the "boys' wear" department. In the sexy fatherhood stakes. They took all these tests to prove it, which was pretty embarrassing. But I reckon I already knew that I was OK after this gorgeous nurse gave me a massage and a talc rub-down a couple of days ago. It wasn't just that it felt good to have a massage (it did), it was the proof that at least that part of me had a future — my pecker wasn't going to shrivel up (like my legs probably will), and boy, have I been sweating on that!

OK, OK. So now let me tell you this excellent story I heard from one of the physios who's working on me in here. It's a very simple story but very deep. That's because it's Zen, right? As in Zen Buddhism. And for a (once) good Catholic boy I sure am starting to pick up a few pointers on this Buddhist thing. More on that later. Anyway, here goes — a story to make a blue Saffy feel better.

There were these two Zen monks on a pilgrimage and they came to a very deep, very wide, very wild river. For a while they walked along beside it, hoping to find some shallows where they could cross. They couldn't find anywhere until finally, near the end of the day, they come upon a rocky ford. "At last," one monk said to the other. "We will be over by nightfall." But just as they were about to cross they heard a faint cry and turned to see a beautiful woman seated on the bank. Now Zen monks are supposed to take no interest in women and remain free of lustful thoughts and be celibate all their lives.

(Sure I'm interested in Buddhism but not becoming a monk, thanks. So relax on that score.)

Anyway, the woman called out again. She was so beautiful and her clothes so alluring that one of the monks hesitated then turned back to her. "How can I help?" he asked.

"I am afraid to cross the river," the woman answered. "I am a noblewoman used to being looked after. My ankles are so fine that if I slip on the loose rocks, I will injure myself. Please, you are so young and handsome and strong, will you carry me across?"

Flattered, the monk did so. When he reached the other side he put the woman down safely on the bank and she kissed him full on the mouth then slipped away without another word. The monks continued on their way, but as darkness fell the monk who had chosen not to help the woman began to slow down and glance back to the river until he finally fell behind his companion.

"Come, come," his friend warned, "or else we will never find refuge by nightfall." Still the monk dawdled.

His friend now noticed that he was looking for something. "What are you looking for?" he asked.

"The beautiful young woman," the monk answered, "I cannot help thinking of her. I was wondering if she was safe."

Then his friend replied, sternly but wisely, "I would not know. I left her at the river. It is clear that you did not."

That's good, hey? It helped me to get rid of some of the anger and guilt and hate that I was starting to build up like pus in my heart and mind. It helped me to leave that behind. To leave it at the river. No, I haven't dumped it all yet, but I'm working on it. And so should you, I reckon.

I heard that story from Jason, one of my physios, like I said. He's more of a counsellor. He's into Buddhism but he's not Asian. He's an Australian of Irish descent. But what he says about life makes sense and it's not all that superstition about candles and crosses that I was brought up on. He has talked about acceptance of our lot and growing through that acceptance. He's talked about suffering in a different way. He told me that he believes the first duty of a human being is to simply play their given role — to simply be, like the sun and the moon, the rivers and the sea, the stars and the clouds. This means living a life without resistance, without faults too, so that the individual can order their mind and identify their consciousness as one with the workings of the universe.

So I'm starting my fight back, Saffy. And you have to as well. My legs are your Aunty Bea. They can make us or break us so we have to "leave them at the river."

You mean an awful lot to me, you know. I really wish that you were here and that I could see you and talk to you and hear you laugh. Mum and dad are OK. So is my little sister. They try. But I've gone beyond them, if you know what I mean, and I'm not being horrible when I say that. I want to find myself now, but I need a shoulder to lean on.

The doctors are saying that I have to start "rehab." I laughed out loud when they told me that. "Rehab to what?' I said. "Modelling?" Ha! "Workshop," they said, so I'm off to play silly sods next week in the "sheltered workshop." I just hope I'm up to it.

Please write — honestly and often — as always, but now more than ever.

He who still returns to the river. Sometimes.

Venny

Letter 27

The Penthouse
511 Park Avenue
New York NY 10017

September 30

Dear Venny

Thank you so much for your quick-as-quick answer to my call for help! Especially when you have so much to face up to for yourself. You are a generous guy, you really are! You've made me feel better — you've even made me laugh! Oh Venny, you are so irreverent! I was thinking that as I read the priest bit, and then I read on and I thought, oh Venny, you are so very reverent! But it's not a contradiction. You revere life — you must — or you wouldn't be trying the way you are to get on with it despite everything — despite rivers and crevasses, the deepest edges.

Yes, I'll try to leave Aunt Bea and Lema at the river, but for the moment I'm still paddling there myself. More about that in a minute.

I'm glad you are so pleased about the "boys' wear" department, as you so delicately put it — the bit concerning the "sausages and olives." Having babies. I've honestly never thought about it much — for me I mean — not until your letter, which made me wonder how I'd feel if I were suddenly told I wasn't ever going to be able to have babies of my own. I guess with a guy, though, it's not only fertility but ability!! Because we all know that sex is more than having babies! I know I wasn't thinking about bambini for one single moment when I was in Cannes — not that I'm going to mention that again! But you know what I mean ... It's good news and I just have the feeling there will be more to come for you.

So much has gone down since Bali, since your accident, since a life ago. Aunt Bea and I have had a heart to heart at last. Not the kind I was expecting, but better than her routine evasiveness.

The last night in PNG, Aunt Bea told me she didn't think it would work with both of us (Lema and me, that is) in New York with her, and I had to agree. Lema is so damn cheerful and nice all the time, it makes me barf!

I've already managed to have a few run-ins with her, and of course Bea always leaps to her defence. Last bitch-up we had, I said some pretty pointed things. I couldn't help myself — it all came pouring out. Hmm, I think I even said something about "gold-digging," which I honestly didn't mean to! Bea really tore into me and told me a few home truths. Funny, I thought she was learning to like, dare I say even to love, me because I sure as hell learned to love her. But it wasn't, isn't, can't be the case. She doesn't love me, not really. And this has been harder for me to accept than any of the other changes about to happen. A betrayal! Another of life's betrayals — like my Mom dying and my Dad.

After her temper with me had cooled that last night in PNG, we talked. It was a pretty honest, pretty painful, talk. She told me how hard it had been for her to suppress all memories of Laurence for all this time. That now, with Lema there, he is by her side too, and all those long lost years have kind of compressed and are at last evaporating. She told me how "blessed" (that was her word) she was to find Laurence's progeny the way she has. She told me she was grateful for my company on her long voyage and hoped I'd learned something! (About the human heart — well, yes!) She also told me she wanted the best for me. (Oh yeah?) Then she told me Lema would be staying in the apartment with her, going to the same school I attended (poor thing), and generally being me, but without all the difficulties I present, no doubt.

Back here in New York I've had time to reflect. I know I haven't exactly been dumped. Not exactly, but it's not a bad imitation, don't you think? You see, Bea says that she'll pay my way through art college, so that's fantastic, because I know I want to do that with a passion. (Not that I've painted or thought about painting for weeks and weeks.)

I asked her point blank though, "If I can't live with you, where will I go?" She patted my arm, oh so comfortingly. In truth I think she was relieved that I didn't kick up a real stink about it, though I felt like it, I can tell you. Dismissed out of hand. Expendable! That's me!

She told me that there's a loft on Grand Street, Greenwich Village, that she's thinking of for me. She knows very well it's a part of town (right near Chinatown and Little Italy) that I absolutely adore. She said that she was "looking into arrangements" for me and that a lot of artists live there and each of them has a shingle outside that says "Artist-in-Residence." She reminded me of this fact as a kind of drawcard, I suppose.

"I've known all along, my dear," she went on, "that the Village is where you'd probably live."

"By myself?" I asked in a panic because, Venny, I suddenly felt so little and afraid and clingy. Even the prospect of the all-white-teeth-and-broad-smiles Lema seemed better than the stillness of alone.

"You can have someone share, I'm sure. Another art student perhaps. Saffron, it's time you went out into the world, don't you think?"

I nodded dumbly and at this moment the smiling Lema appeared and draped her arm round Aunt Bea's neck and — guess what? — attention diverted from me quick-time.

I just sat there staring at the Vuillard and Gaugin paintings that I'd become so accustomed to, saying over and over, "It's all going to change, it's all going to change." (No, I didn't mean the paintings, though I don't expect I'll have a Gaugin on my wall.) And then, Venny, I thought of you and I don't know, somehow, dreadful as it is for you, your whole situation, it gave me courage. You gave me courage. "It's all changing for both of us," I added to myself. "For Venny and me." And I wanted to see you so badly at that moment I felt like nicking some of her jewels and buying an air ticket. I pictured myself breaking into your hospital room ...

Then I looked back at them sitting there, totally engaged in each other. They kind of bill and coo. They whisper and giggle like girlfriends in 4th grade, and it twists something inside me, I've got to admit. I must be the jealous type. So I just got up and walked away and Bea didn't even notice.

I'm to have an apartment, I thought as I went back to my room that is soon to be her room. And a room mate to share. It's not the end of the world. Maybe it's a beginning!

(So, you see, I am pulling away from the river — at least I'm trying to, though I'm not sure if I'm heading for a cold bath under the waterfall!)

What I didn't know until the evening, Venny, and that from a typed-up piece of paper left on my desk, is that the Village apartment is actually mine. Well, it's to be mine when I turn 21, if I do what Aunt Bea has planned for me — that is, complete Art School, and of course I will. It's all I'm clinging onto at the moment, the thought of that. I've worked out that it's a kind of farewell gift from Bea. Sort of like a divorce settlement, I guess. The attorney keeps telling me, "You're such a lucky girl, you know! An apartment on Grand Street and an allowance until you finish your course. You should be very grateful, so lucky, how fortunate, lucky, lucky, LUCKY ... " To which I reply, "And so is Saint Lema of the Smiles, wouldn't you say?"

But to have my own apartment on Grand Street! It's scary. It's strange. It must be good.

On reflection, Venny, I know that I am lucky, though there's this cold fear still creepy-crawling in my gut. A place of my own in a part of town I love. Art school. What more could I want? Well, I do want something more — three guesses what that is?

168

Françoise has proved to be a dear. She said she'd help me set up the apartment, "while your aunt is preoccupied, darling." No doubt Bea suggested that to her (she obviously just wants me out of her hair once and for all), but it's nice to know somebody, somewhere, is still interested in me.

Françoise, old dear, is fun and to tell the truth I think she's a bit scandalized about Lema. She and Bea had their first argument ever because Françoise said if she were Bea, she'd make Lema have a blood test! So Françoise is sort of on my side (the outside).

Kevin phoned me from Bali, too. He said he's not really surprised about the turn of events, but that it's worked out better for me than he imagined. He said I should try to be real cool about the whole change thing, because I would probably have a better time of it than Lema! That amazed me! He was talking about how the "cultural change" for her would be monumental the minute she's away from Bea. Whereas for me, he thinks art is my future and that I'll be free to pursue it now, in a way that Bea would never have let me. That helped, but my heart is still aching and I can't help nasty jibes at Lema whenever I'm with her alone, which is not often.

So that's my news so far.

Zen Buddhism sounds interesting. You are teaching me now, Mr Merlo, because I went to the library and looked up a book on it. I liked what I read, especially the bit about learning and reaching a "higher consciousness." I'm not sure that I understood all of it, but I think it's about the idea of "being" rather than "having?" That goes quite against the grain of

American society, as far as I can see, now doesn't it? Seeking to really know yourself? Discovering Buddhism is something that might never have happened to you if you'd done the modelling thing, you know. Cold comfort, I suppose, but at least it is something positive in all of this.

You know, I keep thinking, if the baby-making department is OK, isn't there a chance that your legs might heal and work again too, given a bit of time and lots of therapy? Think positive. Think brave. Think strong. Think love. Think:

Saffron

PS. And phone me. This is my number:
   +1-212-431-5036.
And guess what? Aunt Bea is arranging a computer for me, so we'll be able to email each other if you can get one!

Letter 28

10 October

Dear Saffy

Jeez, it's great to hear from you. Always great. And getting better too. You know I smell your letters? I do. I used to be good at picking female perfumes before but I reckon I've lost my touch with the antiseptic stink of the hospital seeping into everything. So what is it that I can smell? Is it some rare and exotic fragrance you discovered in India? Or is it New York? Is it the spicy life of the city making its statement even on paper? Or is it you? Is it the heady scent of your skin? Is it? Because that's what I'd like to imagine. OK, OK. Give me a break. I'm a lonely boy. Very lonely, and sometimes my imagination runs riot.

And while I'm on the subject of the imagination, your letters rave on about me so much that you make me blush. I don't deserve all that praise. Don't make me into something that I'm not. I mean, the brave but legless hero thing. And please don't get too excited about the Buddhist thing either. No, I'm not going to get my head shaved (I'm hanging on to every bit of myself that I can these days) and I don't think I'd look too good wearing long flowing robes in a wheelchair. Not really an ethereal image, especially if they get tangled up in the wheels. Besides, and seriously, I just don't have the temperament — I know that I'm far too egocentric to take the beliefs on. I was a model, remember. No, it's just something that I'm exploring.

I have my up days and my down days. The down days are truly terrible. Truly terrible. So if there's something that can give me some direction, I want to know about it.

Still, if you want to believe in me, if it makes you happy to believe in me, go on doing it, please. And if it's important that you keep the hope alive that I'm going to walk again, well, keep hoping — please, please, keep hoping — and praying too, if you are — but don't ask me to. Not right now. I don't know what I believe in any more.

The other day I saw this video called "Hope Floats" (oh yes, we have all sorts of mod cons in here — except for one or two essentials like legs). This movie starred Sandra Bullock (well, not really "starred," since she can't act) and, apart from the fact that it was the most sentimental Hollywood crap I've ever seen, the thought hit me that the expression should be "*!&@ floats," not "hope floats." At least that's what Joel used to say when anything went wrong. Man, do I believe that now, more than ever. The bad memories, the anger just keep on surfacing in my head. I know they're still floating in that river I should have left far behind weeks — no — months ago, but it's just not that easy.

Sorry, Saff. Sorry. Sorry. Sorry. I'm still like that big boil. If you're silly enough to touch me, worse, to squeeze me, all this pus comes out. Horrible image, I know, but it's true. Try as hard as I can, I just can't get rid of the negativity. I am trying with the positive attitudes but the horror still creeps up on me. Saffy, what did I do to deserve this? That's what I want to know. I never hurt anyone in my whole life. And why serve this up when I was just beginning? Why didn't He, They, Them — Whoever — whatever — pulls the strings up there let me have just a bit more of the good life, then take it away — if He, They, Who or Whatever had to?

You get it?

I've got a counsellor appointed to me by the hospital but he's a total jerk so Jason, my physio (he's the Buddhist) has been working on me in the "spiritual" department — actually he calls it my "spiritual journey." That's a bit too "hippy-trip" for me to relate to, but anyway, since I was onto him about the "legless hero" thing (I get told how brave I am 100 times a day), Jason lent me a book called "The Hero with a Thousand Faces" by a guy called Joseph Campbell. The book's about the nature of the hero figure over the ages, especially how the hero is represented in myths. When Jas gave it to me I thought, oh yeah, this is another one of those trendy, touchy-feely, New-Age, pop-psychology books. I've been given stacks of them since the accident (to improve my attitude, self-esteem, will to live, motivation — you name it), like one called "The Road Not Taken" (Chuck! Vomit! You need a bucket and a good tiled floor you can hose off before reading that one!). But the Joseph Campbell book isn't like that. It traces figures like Christ and Buddha and a whole lot of folk heroes, showing that they share similar characteristics in spite of the different ages and cultures that produced them. He points out that there is a sort of standard "Hero Quest" too. He says that we are all potentially our own heroes but we must face the terrors and fears and challenges of the quest if we are going to come through. Like we must face our own worst fears and be stripped of our self-protective devices, until finally we stand naked and alone. It's as if we must die to one world and be born again to the inner world of our true nature.

Yeah, right, I can hear you giggling from across the world. Like Venny's been sucked in badly. Hoot. Hoot. So OK, when I tell it, it does sound like rubbish but it's sensible and true, I think. More important, what I'm saying is that it's the only idea that's keeping me from topping myself right now. It's the only thing that makes sense, that whoever pulls the puppet strings is trying to make me a better person out of all this horror and pus. That there's a point to it. I don't know what the point of letting Joel die so young was — unless maybe he was going to stop taking his tablets and go really crazy and become a mass murderer or something — but I'm finding it hard to shrug it all off and say, "These things just happen." There has to be more to life than random death. Doesn't there?

Although, when I come to think about it, hospitals are filled with random births — three minutes of fun (that's how long it took Joel, he told me!) with no condom — and BINGO — we have random births, so if you can have random birth, why the hell not random death? I mean, if you can be conceived that easily, that carelessly, why not die that easily? I don't know. I'm really wrestling with this. I'm going round and round right now. Round and round and up and down. Highs and lows. I should stop now. Back later.

Later

I've been down to the workshop, which is in a building in the hospital grounds. Since I really should give you some good news, I am an independent wheelie now. My chair is electric and operated from a control panel on the armrest. Just the touch of a finger and whoosh ... Well, nearly ... Anyway, since my arms and shoulders are strong (one good thing that's left from going to the gym 5 days a week before all this), in my upper body I'm still a big boy (and still do weights even now). I can easily hoist myself in and out of bed and into the chair. I can get down to the cafeteria whenever I want for a coffee — but it's not as good as the real coffee shops I got to love from before.

The workshop has been good, I have to admit. First they did all that basket-weaving crap like I was intellectually handicapped, but when they saw I was able to cope and actually produce something when I put my mind to it, they moved me on to jewellery making. Not with jewels, but with rolled or cabochon lapidary stones like agate and carnelian. The metal they set the stones in is Bolivian silver, which sounds expensive but it's pretty cheap if bought in bulk sheets. It's cool to use and looks really smart and very dressy. The hospital board gets in a professional jeweller to run these workshops. Mum and dad have to pay a contribution towards the lessons and the materials. I've still got a fair bit of money saved from before, but they won't let me touch it.

I admit that when I started these workshops I was a real pain in the arse. The instructor's name is Karla and she's very good. Very classy. She designs and produces all her own jewellery under her own name, Karla Larson or KL (her "Maker's Mark" as it's called in the trade). Her work is not like that cheap and tacky costume jewellery — it's beautifully designed on clean and simple lines. Under the circumstances, since she's not a trained social worker or even a teacher, and she's got better things to do with her time than to put up with all the negativity and petty tantrums that I dumped on her, I reckon she's fantastic. Funnily enough, when she found out that I could weld and "had an eye for design," as she calls it, and had mucked about with built sculpture before, she got me going on that again. Only small things.

Remember my jaguar/puma creature? My beggar? Jeez, that's another lifetime. Still, this time I'm going to include the silver and stones in the construction, which I have to say is a buzz. Karla is prepared to take what I do and set up some exhibition space for me in her showroom-gallery. When I get something decent actually finished, that is. The trouble is that, in spite of my best intentions, I often have two or three days in a row when I just can't get myself up. You might think I'm putting on the dog but I just can't.

So, now that all my angst has been worked out and I feel more like a blind pimple than a big pussy boil, finally I can turn to you.

Saff, I have to say that if I was you I would be partying. Forget that stupid cow Bea and that other sap

Lema the Lemming. Boy, is that chick going to find out about life the hard way! I mean, how dumb must she be to trust old Beetroot? But then, maybe they deserve each other — not very Buddhist of me to say so though, hey?

Saffy, more than ever you should get on and forget what is past. You have it all ahead of you. And what a set-up! Even I know what it means to have a pad like that in the Big Apple. And for free. And art lessons. If that's what dumping someone means, I should be so lucky. She's done you a favour. A favour that you should really build on before she changes her fickle little mind again. Go for it. Grab the opportunity with both hands and hold it tight.

You say I should phone you and I would love to but it's not so easy. I'm in a hospital, not at home or a 5-star hotel. I can't just tell the nurse to bring in a phone and let me dial ISD you know. Sure there's a few pay phones in reception but I can't reach the dial from a wheelchair and even if I could I would need a bucket full of change or the world's most expensive phonecard to get through. So, for now, it's still snail mail. It's done us good service so far.

The only thing I ask of you is that you forgive me for being so full of myself right now. I can't help it, honest, but I'm trying. They say that I can go home in 2 to 3 weeks. That will be good but a trauma in itself. The house has no ramps yet and there's toilet and kitchen modifications needed. And there's mum's huge dinners ... sorry! But it will be good to be part of everything there again and dad says he's started cleaning out his

177

old workshop (really a shed) down the backyard to make it into a "studio" for me. So I guess that things can only get better.

Please, please, keep writing and tell me everything the day it happens.

Venero

PS. (Well, not really a PS.) You know, Saff, as I wrote that last line I realized something for the first time. I guess that at nineteen I'm old enough to say it. I just realized that I'm in love with you. I don't really know what I mean by that, but if I'm not, what the hell am I? No joke. I love you. There, I've said it. And boy, does it feel great!

PPS. Now I've said that, don't spit the dummy on me and start thinking that I'm a big jerk starting one of those jail-type affairs. What other guy has a girl he can talk to like I've talked to you? Legs or no legs, I'm one very lucky boy to know a girl like you. Trust me, I'm going to see you one day and if you let me, I'm going to hold you in my arms and cover you with kisses. That's a fact. If you'll let me, that is.

Your special faraway (and very celibate) lover
V.

Letter 29

66 Grand Street
Greenwich Village
New York NY 10013

October 18

Dear Venny

Your letter absolutely bowled me over. I've never had such an admission of love. Never in my life, though various boys have told me sweet lies. And never in writing like that! I was so excited I read your letter and that bit over three or four times before I absolutely took in what you were, what you are saying!

Because, Venny, I know that I love you too. I know I have no need to "swear it," but it seems, given both our situations, that's something I want to do.

I seriously swear my love for you that crosses continents and oceans. There, how's that? It's true.

If Aunt Bea has been searching the world for love, then on my travels with her, I realize, so have I! (Is that a standard 21st-century-type quest, do you think?) The joke is that I didn't even have to leave town to find it, even though you're on the other side of the world.

We were already brought together by one of

those strange life chances. Your funny, rough-and-ready first letter (and let's face it, it was that) had some sort of appeal, as if I knew there was someone there I just might want to get to know better. Maybe it was the same with you, though I blush a bit when I think about telling you to use Spellcheck (not that you didn't need it)! And the fact we've kept writing for so long now, despite gaps of months on end, means there must have been something weird(?) wonderful(?) linking us from the beginning. Something that was/is going to burst into bloom. Weird or wonderful? Who cares!

You say you're lucky to know a girl like me, but I feel so lucky to know you, Venny. You came with me all around the world, long travelogues and all, and guess what, Boy Hero — you're right by me now, you know.

Another thing I figured out this morning, looking back over that swathe of your letters (nearly three years of them and, yes, I've kept them by me, and not as a scribble pad either) — another thing is that I realize we've kind of changed together, haven't we? We were both a bit lost, in a way. We didn't really know what we wanted back then. And now there seem to be things we're working out that are majorly important. Things we can share, maybe? No, things we will most definitely share.

What seems all the more awesome about this mind-blowing emotion I'm experiencing, Venny, is that though we know each other so well, we haven't ever met! Not in the flesh, that is. Other than a few photographs, our view of each other has been through (can you believe it?) the written word! Yet I truly think we've met in the best sense, don't you? Through the mind and the heart, and snail mail — though we both know there's nothing like the REAL THING!

I was going to look up some love poetry (Pablo Neruda, that cool guy from Chile, is my favourite, or even Elizabeth Barrett Browning — the English chick who penned one of the most perfect love sonnets in the world, so they say). But I couldn't find my books, which are still in crates all around the loft. Anyway — feat of memory — I think I can remember the first few lines of the Browning sonnet, so here goes:

"How do I love thee? Let me count the ways.
I love thee to the depth and breadth and height
My soul can reach ..."

Romantic or what?

Now, as my first task in my new home (Grand Street loft, furnished simply with the help of Françoise), I thought I would write you and tell you how much your love is returned. And your kisses. Immediately. Just in plain old Saffy words again.

Over the last 24 hours I've been dreaming of something quite fantastic! Just read on:

(Serious bit!) The hero book sounds inspiring and I agree that we're all on a journey to discover "self." That's not an original idea really (not if you go to a shrink in New York, anyway). But I think, even though people find it easy to blah on about the idea, they don't find it easy to understand — not in the deep, deep sense. I mean, "to stand naked and alone" —

181

NAKED AND ALONE — WOW! I think there are scads of people who've never had that feeling of being "laid bare" — Aunt Bea, for one. She's always distracting herself with people, possessions, travel, more things — when I come to think of it, she's clutching at happiness through other people. She never faces herself, or if she does in those lightning-brief moments, she hides from the glimmer of truth as quickly as she can.

I think Françoise and Kevin are right and Bea'll get tired of Lema, etc., etc. But do you know what? Now that I'm here, I simply don't give a damn! In fact I thank her, I thank them both. This is certainly an excellent chance for me to know more of the "inner world of my true nature," as well as a chance to simply "play." Venny, I somehow know that here, in my own place, I can be light-hearted in a way I can only ever dimly remember.

Sure, I've been forced to face my fears. And even though I feel real desperate sometimes, as you know, those hopeless feelings do pass eventually (though you can feel like an ant in a pile of you-know-what). I'm actually stronger when they've passed. Just as you sound stronger every letter, Venny, you really do!

As for a purpose to everything, hmm — I must say I don't think there's a Master or even a Mistress Puppeteer, Mr Merlo. But I do think we have the power to really imbue (lovely word) meaning ourselves. For me it's through a whole lot of things I'll talk to you about one day, but most of all I figure it's about being connected. That sounds like electric wires — well, there is electricity as far as you and I are concerned, isn't there, Venny?

Hey, I think that's enough on that theme!

(Not so serious bit.) First, did you know that in Hebrew one of the words for "salvation" is also the word for "space?" Make what you will of that! Now let me describe my space. I can't imagine now how I ever had a moment's doubt about this move. It is heaven! I'm ecstatic about the loft, the building, the address. From the funny old goods lift (it was once a warehouse for fabric — big bolts of it) that takes you up to the second floor and deposits you into a large, enchanting space, to my bedroom and bathroom, which Françoise is helping me design to be cleverly screened off as kind of living quarters, to the great high, light-as-light space at the back of the loft which already has my canvasses and all the accoutrements of an artist. Yep, I think I've come to heaven on the second floor.

I feel truly an artist here. I work late into the night and never feel lonely. (So strange! And why I was so freaked out by the idea, I can't imagine now.) What I'm in the process of doing is probably the most important discovery I've ever made about myself in my life (apart from writing you, of course). The future quite suddenly seems much more tangible to me, rosy even. Let me tell you what I'm thinking — in a minute, when I'm done with the loft. I'm trying to paint a picture for you which you won't be able to resist.

The front windows, which have a pretty meagre iron balcony (one person can stand out there, just, but it

183

will take pot plants), look out into the Village and across to a restaurant called Lucky Strike where I'm already getting to know the waiters. No, I don't mean that kind of friendly, but this-is-my-neighbourhood kind of friendly.

What a neighbourhood! Art galleries, book shops, cheap restaurants and super-expensive ones, open-air markets, street sellers, swish clothes shops! Museums. The lot! I've been out running wild exploring everything. There's Mott Street round the corner, with great restaurants and crazy stalls and emporiums, as well as buckets of Chinese vegies to choose from (it's fun haggling over cabbages and bok choy). And then there's Mulberry Street round the next corner, that takes you into Little Italy and the best cappuccinos ever! Then there's the Korean shop a few streets up on Green Street, open until midnight. They sell everything from flowers to fresh veg. to charcoal tablets, should you need them. I love all the Asian ingredients and also the cookbooks I've found round here. Françoise has pronounced my cooking the best she's tasted in a long time. She's inclined to be extravagant in her praise, of course, but to tell you the truth, Venny, I think she's living out her own girlhood kind of freedom thing in this loft. She comes to see me every other day! And I feel sure she's relieved that Bea's not hanging around me any more. We only talk about the future.

I'm even thinking ahead to Christmas when the first Christmas trees come into the Korean shop. I've decided I'm going to buy my own and decorate it, just like Mom and I used to do with our friends from the trailer park. (OK, I have no friends yet to come share Christmas, but I'm sure as hell going to work on that!) I don't know why the thought of the Christmas tree excites me so much — but then again, maybe I do. Maybe I do!

(Extra serious bit!) What do you think of this for an idea? I need a flatmate, Venny, and I'd decided a fellow artist would be groovy! There's still work going on in my loft as far as bathroom and kitchen go. But it would be easy to adapt it for someone in a wheelchair! Françoise agrees — easy as! Venny, why don't you come and live here with me? ("Come live with me and be my love, and we will all the pleasures prove" — poetry, not mine.) I've been asking around and there's some real good work going on with spinal injuries in this country (they say the best in the world in fact), and maybe this could be the chance for intensive therapy. And for intensive therapy of another kind, if you get my drift.

Oh, Venny, when I thought of it I couldn't sleep, and in fact I did some detective work so that I could call you straight away to run it by you. Only to be told by a sleepy nurse that it was the middle of the night in Brisbane, Australia, and no, she wouldn't fetch you, and I should remember it's a hospital and blah-de-blah! So I did the next best thing and wrote you, and I know I'll probably have to wait the two weeks to hear your voice because you'll be home by then. But I'm hoping you'll answer by express as this letter is going express.

I'm longing to hear your voice. I'm aching to hold you close, my darling, darling Venero. I can say that now and will say more, much more! I'm longing to make love to you. Most of all, I'm longing to hear you say yes, yes, YES! There's the rest of our lives to work out everything else. We can do it! So just say it! Yes!

Saffron

PS. My God! I've just twigged that this is a PROPOSAL! Oh well, what the hell, Venny, what the hell!

Letter 30

23 October

Dear Saffy

OK! OK!!!! Man, what news! You're really talking to me now. I mean, really talking! Holy hell, who would have believed that little Miss New York — Miss Richie Rich — would fall for me, the illiterate drip from Springvale? Crazy. It's all crazy. Maybe Father De Lesseps has got a point. Maybe all things do work together for the good, as he used to say (before I told him to get stuffed and say his beads at some other bedside). But it has all worked out for the good, hey, Saff? And you don't know the half of it yet.

First, I go home next week so this might be my last letter. Sigh. Sad but ... then I can phone you, no sweat, and we can talk and talk and I'll lie back on my pillow and imagine you and talk some more — like lovers are supposed to.

Second, we'll have plenty to talk about. My work sold at Karla Larson's Gallery, plus commissions for more, would you believe? And no, it's not a sympathy thing for the poor legless boy-artist. I made it a condition of the show and the sales (if any) that this was never to be mentioned. So they like what I did.

Better, far, far better, Jason — the good physio — and Karla got together and they have found out there's a travelling scholarship for disabled artists on the go.

It's like a Christopher Reeve kind of thing. It's aimed at helping people in circumstances like mine and allowing them money to travel to widen their artistic horizons. The conditions are that you are disabled (natch!) and that you've had at least one one-man show. Karla is going to float that for me, and when I get home and into the workshop Dad has set up in his old shed, I'll really be able to fly.

I love what I'm doing. The stones, the silver — it's all so cool. The clientele is so cool. People with class and good taste. (Natch!) I'm making some jewellery but mostly free-standing sculptures. Not huge. I can't manage anything too big. Usually about 30–50 centimetres high. Constructions of people and animals — some abstract, some close to realistic insofar as the metal I choose will allow. I like using the silver very much. Karla has put me on to that. Sometimes I burnish it to a matt finish, sometimes I polish it. Depends. I am using onyx and marble too, mostly as bases. Very swish. Very classy. Sometimes I laugh, thinking it's all pretty close to panel beating (my boyhood dream), and the truth is that dad does help me with a lot of the tricky welding. His experience is second to none. Still, I've got a lot to learn. And a lot to look forward to.

So, my darling one, I am coming to be with you. True. Silly and impossible as it sounds, I am coming over. And do you know what? Even if the scholarship thing falls through (and both Jas and Karl promise that it won't), well, I'm still coming. Nothing will stop me getting out of this place this time. I've still got my own money and I'll use that. Just let me mount this show and then I'll be out of here.

So, Saffy, you make sure that little ol' apartment is clean and tidy (and roomy) and that the elevator is working (no stairs for this kid) and there's coffee in the pot and a fire in the grate and a rug on the hearth and some soft, soft cushions and ... and ...

Enough already, Saff. I'll phone from home in the next week (unless you beat me to it!! Hint, hint). And I'll see ya in New York.

Love. Life. Love. All to you, for you, from you.

I love you

Always

Venero

Saffron Duval

Venero Merlo

Artists in Residence

Mercy's Birds

Linda Holeman

Mercy is nearly sixteeand a misfit, or at least that's how she likes to appear, but her black dyed hair and black clothes don't fool everyone.

At home, she has to cope with her depressed mother and her eccentric aunt, who is a larger than life fortune-teller and alcoholic. Terrified by the impending return of her aunt's predatory boyfriend, Mercy retreats further behind her image as she tries to maintain the illusion that all is well.

However, Mercy's barriers are gradually eroded by the unexpected friendships with Vince, Mama Gio and Andrea, who see beyond her bleak exterior, and teach her to open up and accept help from others.

"... this is a convincing portrait of a life that is snowbound by circumstance, fear and misplaced independence. And eventually Mercy does find her place in the sun." The *Guardian.*

"I would definitely recommend it to my friends."
Ruth Millican, age 14.

Flyways